"Sure in its emotional footing and c[...] Soul Kiss takes the conventions of the [...] verts them through a richly imagined [...] yet is nuanced and shaded by the [...] When she begins to trust her father, Mariah tells him, 'I want to make words so delicious that people will want to eat them.' Youngblood has more than achieved that goal herself . . . Soul Kiss will make you hungry for more of Youngblood's writing."

—*The Washington Post Book World*

"Extraordinary . . . I suspect Mariah will eventually join the pantheon of young girls coming-of-age that includes Scout Finch (*To Kill a Mockingbird*) and Francie Nolan (*A Tree Grows in Brooklyn*)."

—*Bay Area Reporter*

"Although the quiet and respectable Aunt Merleen and Aunt Faith earnestly try to provide Mariah the structure and advantages that her mother, Coral, could not, Mariah's ability to love and connect with others is stunted. In her heart, she is an abandoned child . . . haunting eroticism, lyrical description and complex characterization . . . gets inside the soul of an acutely isolated girl."

—*Publishers Weekly* (starred review)

"[A] tender, coming-of-age story . . . Set against the tumultuous backdrop of the late 1960s, her novel explores the healing process from family fragmentation through the innocent eyes of Mariah."

—*Essence*

(*continued on next page*)

"Poetic and compelling."

"Youngblood . . . uses language like a painter uses paint, decorating her canvas with color and depth . . . Among the best of Southern storytelling."

"A moody, lyrical coming-of-age drama . . . sensitive and honest . . . [an] intriguing debut."

"A young girl's tale of sadness and longing . . . an erotic odyssey."

"Brutal yet tender . . . [a] moving debut."

"Poetry lovers will appreciate the supple, expanding and contracting medium that Youngblood compounds from everyday speech."

"Captures childhood with a richness and immediacy few contemporary works can match."

# SOUL KISS

*a novel*

## Shay Youngblood

RIVERHEAD BOOKS, NEW YORK

Riverhead Books
Published by The Berkley Publishing Group
A member of Penguin Putnam Inc.
200 Madison Avenue
New York, New York 10016

First Riverhead hardcover edition: May 1997
First Riverhead trade paperback edition: April 1998
Riverhead trade paperback ISBN: 1-57322-658-0

The Penguin Putnam Inc. World Wide Web site address is
http://www.penguinputnam.com

The Library of Congress has catalogued the Riverhead hardcover edition as follows:
Youngblood, Shay.
Soul kiss: a novel / by Shay Youngblood.
p.     cm.
ISBN 1-57322-063-9 (acid-free paper)
1. Afro-American families—Georgia—Fiction.
2. Afro-American women—Georgia—Fiction.
3. Afro-Americans—Georgia —Fiction.
I. Title.
PS3575.08685S68     1997     96-51142   CIP
813′.54—dc21

Printed in the United States of America

10  9  8  7  6  5  4  3  2  1

*for Laura & my father*

# SOUL KISS

# ONE

The first evening Mama doesn't come back, I make a sandwich with leaves from her good-bye letter. I want to eat her words. I stare at the message written on the stiff yellowed paper as if the shaky scrawl would stand up and speak to me. *Mama loves you. Wait here for me.* I want her to take back the part about waiting. After crushing the paper into two small balls I flatten them with my fist, then stuff them into the envelope my aunt Faith gave me after Mama had gone. I feel weak as water and stone cold as I sit with my legs dangling over the edge of the thick mattress on the high iron-frame bed, reading by the dim lamplight. I unfold the tiger-print scarf Mama gave me and lay in its center the good-bye sandwich, a small book of rhymes, a biscuit from dinner wrapped in wax paper, and her pink radio that fits in the palm of my hand. I tie the ends of the scarf twice across the body of my treasures and hold it to my heart. I turn off the light by the bed and make my way across the bedroom in the dark.

I tiptoe down the stairs. When I hit the third step from the bottom the wood complains in the darkness. I drop my bundle and the radio comes alive. Elvis Presley singing "Love Me Tender." Aunt Merleen appears like a giant at the top of the stairs in a red union suit with a pair of men's leather mules on her feet, her fine black hair hidden by a lace night cap. Long and lean with fiery skin the color of Georgia dirt. She has a shotgun in her hands pointed at me.

"Make a wrong move and you're dead. Come stand in the light," Aunt Merleen orders.

Aunt Faith emerges from the darkness like a spirit in a white cotton nightgown, big and wide, silver hair wild around her shoulders. Her plump fingers aim a flashlight at the bottom of the stairs. I step into the circle of light and look down at the radio and the stair that betrayed me.

"Mariah!" Aunt Merleen shouts, as if my name was a crime. I take tiny steps backwards, away from the light.

"Child, where are you going this time of night?" Aunt Faith's voice is soft as Mama's scarf.

"My mama's waiting on me. I'm going home," I say to the bottom of the stairs.

"Why don't you stay here and wait for her," Aunt Faith insists.

"You don't like me. I want my mama," I say quietly.

Aunt Faith throws her enormous weight from side to side as she walks. Huge breasts merge with the rolls of flesh wrapped around her waist. Her thighs and legs are long and solid like the trunks of trees. She is warm beige, the color of my mother's pressed face powder, with long, silver hair. Soft, round, and gray. She comes down the stairs and sits on the bottom step. She speaks to me from a distance. Her voice, sweet and sad, floats to me through the darkness. I almost reach out to her. I need the comfort of arms to hold me.

"We're just old. It's been a long time since we been around children. We'll get used to one another. Come on back upstairs. Your mama 'll be back soon. She had some . . ." There is hesitation between the sweet threads of her voice. "Some business to take care of."

Aunt Merleen, tall and stormy, repeats the word "business," twisting it into a hard question. She sucks her teeth in disgust like my mama would do when she was disbelieving or fed up. I wonder what kind of business would make Mama leave me with these sour old women.

"You're a big girl," Mama often said, with confidence, when she had left me alone in our apartment for a night or two sometimes. She had never left me with strangers. These are her aunts, she had known them all her life, but I've only met them this morning and I don't like them and it seems they don't like me either.

"Let's get something straight. I don't allow Elvis Presley music to play in my house," Aunt Merleen roars. "He told the world the only thing a nigger could do for him was shine his shoes and buy his records when he stole every note he sing from colored lips. Turn that mess off."

She gives me a cold look from way up there at the top of the stairs, then heads off to bed with the shotgun over her shoulder.

I turn off the radio, then collect the book and the biscuit and the sandwich of words. I follow Aunt Faith back upstairs one sad step at a time and into the room I am to sleep in. I sit on the bed, grinding

the biscuit between my fingers until it is fine as dust, letting it fall
onto the slip of brown wax paper. I sprinkle the crumbs around the
bed so that any ghosts that might come in the night will eat them and
not bother me in my sleep. Mama taught me to do this after countless ghosts had slipped past the salt sprinkled across our doorways
and windowsills to interrupt my dreams. Mama believes in spirits and
knows their ways. After a while I lie down on the bed with the scarf
across my face, breathing in the bergamot smell of my mother's hair,
tasting bitter tears. I take small bites of the sandwich, careful to taste
every word she left me, even the ones I don't understand, then swallowed each with a tear or two.

When me and Mama lived together the world was a perfect place
to be a little girl. I adored Mama and she adored me in return. No one
else mattered. One of my first memories was watching her dress for
work. Next to her reddish-brown skin, softened each night with a thin
layer of Vaseline and cold cream, she wore a pink satin slip. Pink was
romantic, she said, the color of love and laughing. Mama's slanted eyes,
a gift, she said, from her Cherokee grandfather, were dreamy remembering how my father told her she looked like a princess when she wore
pink. On the outside she wore white. Her nurse's uniform was starched,
white-white, a petite size eight, with a tiny white cap perched on her
short, tight, nappy curls, dyed blonde not quite down to her dark roots.
White silk stockings veiled her long thin legs. Silent crepe-soled white
shoes she'd let me lace up held her perfect, size six feet. Every weekday
morning, on her way to the military hospital, she would walk me to
school past the gray army barracks to the steel, bread-shaped huts,
where we lined up for the pledge of allegiance to the flag.

Armed with a sandwich, a piece of fruit, and a word written on a
small square of pink paper folded twice, I was ready for anything. The

word was written in blue ink in my mother's fancy script . . . *pretty . . . sweet . . . blue . . . music . . . dream . . .* Sometimes she gave me words in Spanish . . . *bonita . . . dulce . . . sueños . . . agua . . . azul . . .* The word I kept in my mouth, repeated like a prayer when I missed her. Mama told me that she would be thinking of the same word all day. That thought made our time apart bearable. Before she left me at the door of the school she would whisper the word into my ear. I'd close my eyes and she would kiss me quickly on my neck, then let go of my hand. She always watched me through the window as I walked to my seat near the back of the room. We would mouth our word to each other once more before she disappeared. When Mama came for me in the afternoon I would take her hand and swing our arms as if we were both little girls on a walk.

"Blue. B-L-U-E. Blue is the color of sad music. Blue." I would pronounce, spell, and give the meaning of our word. Sometimes on our walks we invented words and spoke to each other in new languages. As praise, Mama would tickle me under my chin, then cup my face in her warm delicate hands and close her eyes. She would press her lips full on mine and give me what she called a soul kiss. My whole body would fever from my mother's embrace.

"I love you, Mama," I would say, looking into her eyes.

"I love you more," she answered every time, looking deep inside me.

I could read books before I could walk, Mama said. By the time I was three years old I was sitting on her lap reading to her from the newspaper. I don't remember all this, but Mama said it's so. I was so smart I got special treatment in school. "Teachers' pet" they called me, and other names I grew to hate. I didn't make friends, but I didn't need them, I had Mama. All my days at school were spent passing the time, waiting for Mama to free me from the steel breadbox. She taught me all the important things there were to know.

We lived on a military base near Manhattan, Kansas. Flat squares of grass occupied by long flat gray squares of apartments one after the other for miles and miles. There was a swing in our backyard where Mama spent hours pushing me into the sky. Sometimes I sang songs into the wind, catching pieces of cloud in my throat and swallowing them for safekeeping.

We lived in a tiny apartment. The bare walls were an unpleasant weak shade of green transformed at night by Mama's colored light bulbs into a pink velvet womb. In the living room an overstuffed red crushed velvet sofa sat in the middle of the room on gray-flecked linoleum tiles. There was a table at one end of the room and a lamp with a red-fringed shade and a big black radio on top of it. The radio's antenna was wrapped with aluminum foil so we could get better reception for the blues and jazz music that came on in the evening from someplace so far away that pulsing static accompanied each song. Mama kept the plain white shades pulled down past the window sills "to keep our business to ourselves," she said. The living room opened onto the kitchen where a bright yellow and pink flowered plastic tablecloth was spread over a wobbly card table surrounded by three silver folding chairs. A bare white bulb hung from the center of the white ceiling. White metal cabinets lined one wall and underneath them, an old-fashioned double sink with one side deeper than the other. Mama said she used to wash me in the deep part of the sink when I was small enough to hold in one hand. It always made me laugh when she said that because I couldn't imagine being that tiny. Sometimes I wished I were small enough to crawl back inside her stomach where she said I was once small enough to fit. I could imagine no greater comfort. The bedroom was just big enough to fit the queen-sized bed and chest of drawers which held all our neatly folded clothes among fragrant cedar balls. A clean white tiled bathroom had a toilet that ran all night and a sink that dripped but also a deep, creamy white enamel tub that was big enough to fit me and Mama together just right.

At night we would eat directly from tin cans heated on a one-eyed hot plate while we listened to music on the radio. In summer she said it was too hot to light the oven, in winter she said she was too tired to cook. On special days we had picnics, selecting cans of potted meat, stewed tomatoes, fruit cocktail, applesauce, and pork and beans to spread on saltine crackers or spear with sturdy toothpicks and wash down with sweet lemon iced tea. Mama just didn't have any use for cooking and I never missed it because this was all I knew. After supper we would take a bath together, soaping each other with a soft pink sponge. Sometimes she let me touch her breasts. In my tiny hands they felt like holding clouds must. Like delicate overripe fruit. Her nipples were dark circles that grew into thick buttons when I pressed them gently as if I were an elevator operator. I kneeled in the warm soapy water between her legs letting water pour over her breasts from between my small fingers and watched her as she leaned back in the tub, her narrow eyes closed, hair damp and matted, mouth slightly open as if she were holding her breath. I felt so close to her, as if my skin were hers and we were one brown body. She didn't seem to mind my curious fingers touching and soaping every curve and mystery of her body. There were no boundaries, no place I could not explore. After our bath we lay on the sofa in our clean white pajamas, listening to the radio until we fell asleep. I loved sleeping with her warm belly pressed into my back, one arm across my waist. Sometimes she would hold my hand as we slept.

On weekends me and Mama played Ocean. Around bedtime she would get dressed in beautiful clothes and go out dancing. She left me alone with instructions to stay on the sofa, warning me that if I got off, even to go to the bathroom, I might drown in the ocean. She gave me toast left over from breakfast which I tossed bit by bit to the sharks in the dangerous waters all around my island so they wouldn't nibble on my toes when I slept. I remember a pink lamp with a pink bulb burning and the radio turned down low. A few drops of scotch and lots of pink punch swirled in a chipped blue china cup burned sweetly in my throat. I drifted further out to sea than I imagined I could swim. The sharks began to circle as my eyelids dropped and the horizon across the ocean grew hazy. The sound of small waves rocked me like arms into the deepest part of sleep. Usually I began dreaming right after Mama left.

*I look like my mother. My hair is dyed blonde, my eyes are narrow, shaped like almonds and lined in black ink. My lips are rich with soft, pink kisses. Her hair. Her eyes. Her lips. I even have my mother's breasts. Her thick, delicious nipples. In my favorite, secret dream I dress in her clothes, tight-waisted, sparkly, pink dresses, and dance in a circle of light. I dance until my feet become so light that I float across the dance floor, up toward the ceiling of moving stars, then fly out of my window into other oceans.*

Mama was always there when I woke up. One time she woke me in the middle of the night crying. She told me that a special friend of hers, a hospital doctor, was being sent overseas and because Mama wasn't his wife—he had one already—she couldn't go. Because Mama was sad, I was sad. Her tears were mine. When Mama was crying, it seemed as if the whole world were crying.

Before long, right out of the blue, Mama began to change. I was scared and confused. After school I wanted to tell her about my new classmates in second grade: the Korean girl who put her hands to her face and cried quietly all day; the red-haired, blue-eyed boy from Arkansas who talked like he had rocks in his mouth; the dark-skinned, wide-eyed girl named Meera with clouds of jet-black hair she let me touch at recess and whose mother was an Indian from India. I had a new friend, new books, and a new teacher, but Mama wasn't interested in any of it. She seemed to be sleepwalking through our lives. More and more I was in charge. She let me do everything. In the afternoons I led us home. Her movements became slower, she walked as if strong hands gripped her ankles. Her eyes were dull and her voice weak. Sometimes she wouldn't speak to me, but would mouth our word for the day while I untied her shoes and kneaded feeling back into her toes. I unhooked the stockings from their garters, rolling the silk carefully down her exhausted legs. She would fall asleep, and I would fill a small blue pan with warm water and soak her feet, massaging them gently. I would unbutton her white uniform and hang it in the closet. The wig she had started wearing was curly and dark. I would slide it off her head and place it on its stand. I would take a comb and scratch the dandruff from her scalp, oiling it with bergamot while she dozed, wondering why her hair had begun to fall out. It was dry and coarse and no longer blonde. I would watch her, slumped into the sofa in her pink satin slip, watching the rise and fall of her breasts. Curling up in her lap, I would smooth the satin over the rise of her breasts with both my hands pressing the shape of her body from shoulders to waist, over and over again. Her eyes stayed closed, her breathing raw and hollow. Sometimes Mama would sleep for whole days when she wasn't working. When she woke up she wanted water. Cool water.

Mama had an answer for everything even when she didn't know.

"Where is my father?" I would ask her in the lazy pink light before we fell asleep at night.

"In Mexico, painting the sky blue." She drew pictures with her answers.

"Is he handsome?" I asked, secretly hoping for more.

"Very handsome. You have your father's hands," she'd say, kissing my fingers, each one.

Her voice was twilight, and the stories she told me about him sounded like fairy tales that found their way into my dreams. Did I remember them or did I dream them? She never spoke of him outside of these times between waking and dreaming.

I would close my eyes to listen, seeing every detail, my imagination filling in all the blank spaces.

"How did you meet him? Tell me everything about him," I demanded. Mama closed her eyes and drifted beyond my reach. She tossed me bits of stories to nibble on. I devoured the nights, the days of her memories, growing fat from their richness. The details of her stories changed over time. The season, the city, the natural disaster that took place the day they met, the color of his eyes.

"I was happy then," she would begin each time. "I was so happy then."

One legend began: "It was springtime, in California. A light breeze was blowing off the ocean. I had just come on duty when he walked into the emergency room. A cut from his head was bleeding. He had fallen off a ladder. There was pale blue paint all over his face and arms. I thought he had fallen from the sky, he was so beautiful, like an angel. His eyes were so black, I was afraid I would be hypnotized by them. I was taking his blood pressure when the room started to slip sideways. The earth shook me like a nervous child, and I fell into his wide, blue arms. My mind was racing so fast I could see through him. I could see you. Me being earth and him being sky, I knew we would have an angel child. And we did. I wanted to name you Angelita, Walks with Angels, but he said no, so we called you Mariah after his mother."

Other times the story went: "It was winter in New York. It was so cold the day I met your father, my eyelashes froze, and he melted them with his breath."

Sometimes in her memory, they discovered each other on a windswept Caribbean beach: "Your father was at the top of a tall ladder the first time I saw him. A strong wind blew him right into my arms. When we first met, he painted pictures of me every day. Orange bodies with yellow faces, purple arms and red hair. He drank raspberry beer and rubbed my feet with mint leaves. When I met your father there was a strong wind in my hair twisting my mind like a hurricane."

In my mother's stories my father was always handsome and always,

always there was pale blue paint all over his face and arms. I grew to love him too.

At school, me and my friends Meera and David, the blue-eyed boy from Arkansas, played Army during recess. We invented wars and fought against invisible armies of dragons and sea creatures. We always won by the time recess was over and what I liked most was that we were always on the same side.

Mama's beautiful blue script was replaced by shaky, uncertain block letters written in pencil or with a broken red crayon. The words on the slips of paper began to change. *Vieja . . . lluvia . . . vé vé . . . la-grimas . . . mohosas . . .* x's and o's. Once she filled a small square of paper with z's and q's. Sometimes the paper was wet with her tears. Her writing became hard to read, the lines, no longer separated or curved, going nowhere. She seemed hurt and nervous, as if she were afraid of everything. One morning she forgot to give me a word altogether. When I reminded her she pulled a torn scrap of paper from the pocket of her uniform. Her fingers were trembling and couldn't hold the pencil I gave her, so she pressed the paper to her lips twice, then crushed it into my hand. At lunchtime, after eating the slice of dry bread and bruised banana in my lunch bag, I unfolded the paper Mama gave me and pressed it to my lips. I closed my eyes and tried to feel the warmth of her paper kisses.

One time Mama took me to the hospital where she worked. I waited out in the emergency room. One of the nurses gave me a lollipop and asked me if I could do any of the new dances. I said, "No, but I can sing." I stood up on a chair and opened my mouth. I don't know why Billie Holiday came out. "God Bless the Child" haunted the air. Sometimes Mama sang it when she was sad. The nurses and some of the sick people clapped when I was done. Mama's doctor friend was there; he said it sounded like there was an angel in my throat. I explained to him that I put clouds there for safekeeping. He said I was just like my mother. I liked him even though he was the one my mama always seemed to be crying about. I let him kiss me because Mama said it was all right. Up close he smelled sweet, like a woman not my mother.

*I*t was April by the time we left Kansas. I was sure I'd miss ice cream floats at the commissary, swinging into the sky, and my friends Meera and David, but I was hoping what I missed most would come back, the sound of Mama laughing. The day we left, Mama picked me up from school just after lunch. She was wearing a tiger-print scarf tied under her chin, her eyes hidden by large dark glasses. She wore a capped sleeved navy blue dress that showed off her figure. White buttons shaped like little boats floated down the front of the dress to the hem just below her knee. The dress was so tight across the front I could see flashes of her pink satin slip between the buttons when she breathed. She wore dark stockings with runs in them, and scuffed black high-heeled pumps. A hard green suitcase, her red sweater and her box-shaped fake alligator purse were in one hand, my hand was in the other. We were going to take the train to Georgia. She put five kisses in my pocket.

Buildings, gates, and sidewalks rolled behind us. I only looked back once as we were leaving the base on a big green bus. I waved good-bye as if my friends could see me. The huge flag we pledged allegiance to every morning was flapping in the wind halfway down the pole in an enormous blue sky. I saw two soldiers salute each other in front of the library. If we hadn't been leaving it would've been a perfect day. Mama said somebody important had died. She was crying so hard I thought she knew this Martin Luther King, Jr., personally.

"Mama, why we leaving here?" I asked as we boarded the train at the station.

"We ain't leaving, we going someplace else," she said sadly.

"Why, Mama?" I whined.

After a long silence she said, " I like to travel."

Mama let me sit by the window. Small towns and big cities spread out before us. I saw a sign that read: YOU ARE LEAVING THE SUNFLOWER STATE. One station after the other. Babies cried and newspapers rattled open and shut. The train's rhythm rocked me to sleep and shook me awake. The tall, bony conductor whose broom-colored hair stuck out from under his gray hat like stiff toothpicks smiled at Mama with crooked teeth and winked at her. Mama gave him her ticket without even looking up. People got on and off the train. They hugged good-bye and kissed hello outside my window. The new conductor's smooth brown face leaned in close and he whispered to Mama that we'd crossed into Mississippi. We had to change our seats twice. Mama said the view was better, but I didn't like riding backward or sitting next to the toilet. I wondered who would be waiting for us at the end of our ride. I kept looking out the window until all I could see was me, and Mama's reflection sipping ladylike from a big, brown medicine bottle she kept in her purse.

TWO

hen our train rolled into Georgia, Mama woke me up. WELCOME TO THE PEACH STATE. Tall green trees and red dirt. Rusty piles of metal in unmarked fields of car graveyards. Coke machines sat on the front porches of little wooden houses that looked about to fall down. Mama looked scared. She started talking as if she was trying to convince me of something. She left spaces wide enough for me to ask questions, as if I knew enough to ask the right ones. Her voice changed. She sounded different, almost like a little girl. She sounded as if she believed half of what she was telling me. She offered her words to me like sweet poison.

"I'm gonna take you to visit your great aunties. Aunt Faith and Aunt Merleen. You be nice. You be nice, you hear? Do what they tell you." She licked her pointing finger and used it to brush down my eyebrows. "They're strict, but they're good people. I used to stay with them when I was little. They like things clean."

I squinted as she picked sleep out of the corners of my eyes.

"I would stay with my aunties when my mama had to go work on Saturday nights and sometimes when she'd go down to Florida to pick fruit I'd stay with them all summer. They was some kinda nice. They're ladies . . . and they know how to cook." Mama stopped talking and looked out the window like she was remembering and seeing at the same time all their niceness. Her eyes were hungry—maybe she was looking forward to a plateful of something good.

"Maybe they'll teach you how to cook a red velvet cake or a blackberry cobbler. I haven't had a cobbler since . . . oh, I don't know when. They sure do know how to cook. Oh, and Aunt Faith, she play the piano. Maybe she'll teach you how. She only plays classical music, though, and church songs."

Mama's smoky voice whispered pieces of a song, *"The cares of the world may leave us crying. . . . Life will be sweeter some day . . ."* Her voice trailed off into a hum. Even when I couldn't hear it anymore, I could still see the song swaying in her body.

"They got a big fine house, them two. They'll be nice to you. You'll see. They'll be nice." Mama got busy taking my hand in hers and rubbing it against her face. I wondered why they had to be so nice to me.

"Mama, why you crying?" I got scared and pressed my hands to her face and neck to soak up her tears.

"I'm happy. We're almost home," she said, gently putting my hands back in my lap. She stopped talking. Her face didn't look happy, it cast a stony gaze on the landscape outside the window.

Gradually, small broken houses leaning so close they seemed to be listening to one another rolled beside us. The train crawled into the town where my mother grew up. The train station was just a raised platform by the side of the road. Nobody was there to meet us. Mama went over to a yellow taxi and asked the driver if he could give us a ride. The man said something to Mama that made her jump away from the cab as if she had been bit by a snake. Mama called him an "ignorant cracker." She was mad, but she wouldn't tell me why. Another woman with long red hair and pretty white teeth got in the cab and they drove away in a cloud of dust. Mama took off her high heeled shoe and threw it at the cab, then she sat on the curb and started to cry.

"It's okay, Mama. We can take another train somewhere else," I said, sitting down next to her.

"No, baby, we at the end of the line," she said, limping after her shoe.

Mama took my hand and we followed the train tracks for a long time until we started seeing people. Friendly faces, all smiles, some waved, some hollered out a "Good morning." I asked Mama if she knew all these people and she said, "No, folks just friendly down south." I started waving and saying good morning to people I didn't even know. We passed a red brick school building with a flag waving out front, a grocery store, a liquor store, and some long wooden houses Mama said were shotgun houses. Finally we came to where we seemed to be going. Mama stood looking at the big white house in front of us, then she spit on her handkerchief and wiped my face. She brushed my hair back with her hand. When she was satisfied she adjusted her scarf and we walked past the tall, black gate.

Coming up the neat brick walk lined with flowers, we saw the lace curtains move away from the window and fall back again. Mama walked quickly up the steps dragging me along.

"Aunt Faith, Aunt Merleen, this is my little girl, Mariah. She's seven years old and already she can sing like an angel," Mama announced loudly to the closed door. "Sing, baby," she said to me.

Mama was anxiously squeezing my hand. It hurt a little, but I didn't say anything. I kept my eyes low, on the dusty points of Mama's shoes. I had a bad feeling in the bottom of my stomach. Before I could open my mouth, I heard the door open and looked up to see two old women looking back at us.

Through the screen Aunt Merleen looked me over like I was a spoiled ham, then turned and went deep inside the house. The other one, Aunt Faith, seemed afraid to let us cross the threshold into the big white house with the ocean-blue porch ceiling and tall shuttered windows.

"We haven't seen you in quite some time, Coral," the soft, round one said accusingly.

"You been to see your mother?" the tall, stormy one demanded from inside the darkness.

"Not yet," Mama answered timidly. There was a long, sweaty silence. Mama dabbed at her neck with the ends of her scarf and fussed with my collar. We stood there, shifting from foot to foot, waiting for a sign of welcome.

"Sure is hot!" Mama said at last.

Aunt Faith said something to the tall one behind her, then opened the screen door reluctantly to let us pass. It was cool and dark inside. I held on to Mama's dress like I did in a crowd so we wouldn't be separated. We followed Aunt Faith into a large room with heavy drapes on the window. We sat on an uncomfortable high-backed sofa covered in an itchy wool fabric while Aunt Faith sat across from us in a matching chair.

"I need to talk to you, Aunt Faith. I'm in trouble."

Aunt Merleen came into the room and stood by the large black piano.

"Coral, seems like you always in some kind of trouble. Didn't you leave here under a dark cloud?" Aunt Merleen's rough voice filled the room.

I sat on Mama's lap and tried to unbutton her dress so that I could find some comfort against her pillows of softness, but she pushed me away.

"The child look too big for that." The rough voice clouded my ears.

Under their scrutiny I felt shame for the first time. I began to shrink to the size of a baby that would fit into the palm of my mother's hand. Mama folded my hands in my lap and buttoned her dress in the wrong hole. Then Mama took off her scarf and gave it to me. She cupped my face in her hands and kissed me on the lips. She held me too tight, then stood up and stepped away from me, looking at me as if she were trying to take a picture. Her eyes were sad and wet. She started crying out loud, then left the room with Aunt Faith's hand on her shoulder. Me and Aunt Merleen stared at each other until I backed down and started looking at the pattern in the carpet, counting the flowers along the border under my feet.

"Can you talk?" she shouted, as if I were deaf.

"Yes," I whispered.

"Yes, what?"

"Yes, I can talk." I dared to look into her rough and wrinkled face, the light-colored eyes, the wide flat nose and small tight mouth.

"Yes, ma'am. Didn't your mother teach you any manners?" she asked accusingly.

I turned my eyes back to the maze of flowers blooming on the carpet inches below my feet. I tried to think of words to defend my mother. I pressed my hands against my middle and tried to push the pain out of my stomach. Suddenly I heard a door slam and the sound of Mama's high heels running down the front porch steps. I slid off the couch scratching the palms of my hands on the bumpy fabric and ran to the door, but it was shut, locked tight. The hard green suitcase was all that was left of Mama.

"Where's my mama?" I asked the closed door, panic bubbling in my chest.

"She had to go somewhere. She'll be back. She'd like you to stay with us for a while. We want you to stay," Aunt Faith whispered to my back. Her voice was the only one I heard. I wanted to cry, but I didn't. I went back to sit on the sofa and pretended me and Mama were playing Ocean.

*My father is in Mexico painting the sky blue, but I am lost in a forest of dark trees. Trees so tall and dark the sky is not visible. The trees begin to sing to me in Spanish. I sing too, even though I don't know the words. I see a light in front of me and walk toward it. After walking for what seems like days I come to a place where two witches are sitting around a fire. They tell me that they have been waiting for me, that they are going to chop me up into little pieces and boil me into a soup to feed their dead children. One of the witches holds me by my arms while the other one plucks out my eyes. I scream but no sound comes out of my mouth.*

When I fell off the sofa, I found myself drowning in the ocean of thick red flowers.

While waiting for Mama to come back, I pretended that my aunts wanted me to live with them. I pretended that I had somewhere else to go, but I didn't. I pretended that we all had a choice in the situation. I didn't want to follow them up the carpeted stairs and down the hall to the room they told me used to be my mama's but I did, letting my feet drag along. It was a pretty room. Starched flowered curtains framed the window beside the bed and a bright-colored patch quilt covered the iron-frame bed with a mattress so high I had to crawl up onto it. Facing the foot of the bed there was a small white chest of drawers with a plain round mirror hung above it, tilted down so that I could see the wide empty bed behind me. I knew that I would be lonely in that bed, but I had no way of knowing how the pillows would suffer my tears, fists, and teeth marks in the years ahead. Fine lace material covered the surface of the bureau and the small bedside table like altar cloths. Clean, white, and free of any sentimental objects. My aunts talked to me, telling me things I didn't even try to remember because I didn't expect to stay long. I clutched Mama's scarf in my hand, rubbing it against the inside of my arm like a salve. I was hot and hungry and my arms itched. I didn't see Mama's suitcase, but the clothes we'd packed in it were folded neatly on a chest underneath the window. My book of rhymes sat on top of the small pile and I stared at it, repeating each rhyme I knew by heart.

"Do you want something to eat?" the tall one asked me. I bit my lip to keep from crying. My insides felt like an empty echo.

"There's something on the stove. Come on downstairs," Aunt Faith took my hand and led me down the back stairs to the kitchen. I washed my hands in the sink. She put a warmed-over chicken leg and a biscuit on a pretty little pink plate and placed it in front of me. To the left of the plate a white paper napkin was folded into a triangle and on it laid a shiny silver fork. A short glass of milk and a knife were on the right. The two old women sat down at the table and watched me as I picked up the piece of meat with both hands. Just as I was about to take a bite, Aunt Merleen said, "Don't you say grace before you eat?" I put the chicken back on the little pink plate and watched them close their eyes and pray over the food. I waited until they started eating before picking up my fork. I ate slowly and carefully, watching them watch me. It was the best and the worst meal I'd ever eaten. The best tasting, but without Mama, the flavors were meaningless to me.

"When you get done, put the bones in one of those plastic bags over there. Rinse your dishes and leave them in the sink, I'll do them later," Aunt Faith said, pushing her bulk away from the table.

"She left you this." The tall one dropped a small envelope next to my plate. A letter from Mama. My name was written on the envelope in her hand. My aunts left me sitting alone at the table. I could hear them whispering in the other room, but I kept my eyes on the letter. I couldn't eat the biscuit for thinking about Mama and wanting her to come back soon.

Our routine changed little that first spring and summer. At five A.M. Aunt Merleen started coughing, then her heavy feet would hit the hardwood floor like a clap of thunder. A few minutes later I could hear the water for her bath, then her deep bass singing the blues. Aunt Faith's flannel slippers would shuffle past my door and down the stairs. Tea kettle whistling like a train. Two hard tap, taps on my door. Aunt Merleen hollering up the stairs for me to "rise up." Grits with butter. Buttermilk biscuits. Strong black coffee for them, and for each of us a short glass of carrot juice, a whole garlic clove, and half a dozen colored vitamins. Aunt Faith believed in the power of vitamins and herbs to cure all things real and imagined. Did she think her herbs would cure my memory and bad dreams? I washed myself every morning, missing my mama's hands caressing every plane and crevice of my body with a soapy cloth, then pouring warm water over my shoulders as I stood in the small tin tub in our kitchen. Mama was with me always, it seemed, whispering, touching, and telling me things. Not a day passed that I did not expect her to walk into the room as if she had never left.

Aunt Merleen believed that idle hands were the devil's playthings. She kept me busy gardening. At first I would sit on the back porch watching her spread manure and plant seeds. She wore overalls and rubber boots. Sometimes she would call out for me to bring her a tool or a packet of seeds or a glass of water left on the porch by Aunt Faith.

"Stick your finger in deep as it'll go," she said, pointing to a mound of dirt.

I looked at her as if she had two heads.

"I said come over here and plant something. Pick out something and you can watch it grow." She talked to me as if I were a scared dog.

I hesitated, then finally chose a packet with bright red tomatoes on the cover. Every morning after that I watched and waited for things to grow.

"You can water something, but you can't make it grow," Aunt Merleen would say to no one in particular. "You got to tend to it."

Secretly, I planted words written on scraps of paper. I tended them, spoke to them, and waited for things like *love* and *pink, music* and *Mama* to grow between the rows of leafy vegetables. The first summer I lived with my aunts the garden was flooded by a week of constant rain. I had hoped that my words would take root but I realized that I'd have to start all over again. We heard on the news that it rained so hard coffins were washing up on Main Street. I wondered if it was raining where my mama was.

We ate dinner at noon. Vegetables from the garden, cornbread, and stewed or baked meat. They started to notice my clothes getting smaller. Aunt Faith sewed simple summer dresses for me. After dinner we all took naps. There were music lessons, which I hated, on the big black piano. Aunt Faith loved classical music and was determined to make me love it too. It was different from the blues and jazz wrapped in soft pink lights I was used to. I began to make my own music. When I saw the color blue I would give voice to throaty moans that summoned the ghost of Billie Holiday. There was a small black-

and-white television on a rolling table in a corner of the living room. The tv was only used to watch Walter Cronkite report the six o'clock news or see colored people like Aretha Franklin and Sammy Davis, Jr., singing and dancing, or men walking on the moon, or as Aunt Merleen thought, "walking around in the desert outside of Las Vegas." "God no more put a man on the moon than he made it out of cheese," she said the night of the big event. Mostly the tv was silent beneath a veil of flowered lace.

After evening supper Aunt Merleen would read out loud from *Reader's Digest* or the seed catalog. They ordered exotic flowers and giant vegetables for the garden and family magazines to improve our minds. When her eyes were tired Aunt Merleen made me read. I didn't mind so much because words and reading reminded me of Mama. When I had a choice, I read from the book of rhymes Mama left me, but usually they selected long poems from slim leatherbound volumes by men and women they told me were colored like us. Claude McKay, Langston Hughes, Robert Hadyn, Gwendolyn Brooks, and Georgia Douglas. There were no pictures of these poets but from their words I could tell that they were like me. They wrote about the blues, loneliness, love, bitterness, pain, all about being colored. Sometimes I stole one of the books and slept with it under my pillow so I could dream special dreams. Sometimes I tore pages from the books and ate the poems word by word to keep them inside me.

By eight o'clock the big white house was asleep. Its long blue shuttered windows closed, its patterned carpets free of footsteps. I listened to soul music with the pink radio pressed to my ear until I fell into dark dreaming. Being chased by faceless spirits, being lost, being alone inside the hollow of trees. I'd wake up crying for my mother, then my heart would break remembering she wasn't there. Lying in the dark, I'd try to remember every word my mother gave me until I fell asleep again . . . *green* . . . *heart* . . . *dance* . . . *circles* . . . *la luna* . . .

*T*he first Sunday that comes around Aunt Faith walks into my room carrying a frilly yellow dress across her arm.

"We going to church this morning. Hurry up and get dressed." She lays the dress on the bed and disappears back down the hall. I sit up in bed looking at it. I touch it, so soft and light. Mama used to take me to the commissary to pick out my own clothes and I usually chose uniforms that made me look like a soldier. Beige corduroy, dark wool, and green khaki jumpers. I always got my way and wore what I wanted. I sniff at the dress. It smells like Aunt Faith, musty and sweet. I am sitting on the bed staring at the dress when Aunt Faith sticks her head in the room again.

"Child, that dress is not going to leap off the bed and onto your body. We going to church today."

"We don't go to church," I say, pulling the covers up around me.

"We do in this house. Now put that dress on and let's go," she says, putting her hand on her hip.

I don't move. "Don't you like the pretty dress?" Her voice is higher, expectant.

"I don't wear dresses like that," I say, hugging my knees close to my chest, digging my heels further into the mattress.

"All little girls wear dresses to church on Sunday," Aunt Faith says, moving into the room.

"What's her name?" I ask, touching the ruffles at the hem of the dress.

"Her name?" Aunt Faith sits at the foot of the bed facing me. Tiny beads of sweat are beginning to appear on her top lip and roll down the edges of her plump, gently powdered face.

"The little girl who used to wear that dress." I lift the hem of the dress as if a tiny little girl might still be inside of it. The material swishes like two records rubbed together.

"Her name was Grace, I think. Our neighbor Mrs. Williams works for her family. She outgrew it, but I think it'll be just right for you. Mrs. Williams sent you a big box of clothes and a few books and things too. You can look at the rest of the things when we get back from church." Aunt Faith picks up the dress and holds it against my body.

"Let's see what it looks like on you," she says.

"Is she dead?" I ask. At the hospital where Mama worked there was a box of dead children's clothes. She told me never to wear the clothes of a dead person or I might suffer in my dreams or be haunted by their spirit if the dead person saw me wearing their clothes. I had to be sure.

"No. She's all grown up and can't use them anymore. She's not dead," Aunt Faith says, still holding the dress. I am not convinced.

Aunt Merleen's impatience fills up the the doorway.

"We gonna be late messing around with that child. If she don't want to go leave her here."

"We can't leave the child here by herself," Aunt Faith says, heaving herself off the bed.

Aunt Merleen turns to me as she pins up her fine black hair into a bun. "Put that dress on *now*," she shouts.

I am so surprised I fall off the bed. I'm not hurt, but I whimper a bit and Aunt Faith comes over to comfort me.

"I don't want to be late for service," Aunt Merleen says as she leaves the room.

I am suddenly afraid they are the witches in my dream. Afraid they will boil me in a soup and Mama will never find me. After washing up I put on the dress and hope that no little girl's spirit recognizes me in her yellow dress.

When Aunt Faith brushes my hair too hard, I start to cry, but I don't say anything. I write down every hard word they give me in my memory, every mean thing they do so I can give a full report to Mama when she gets back.

I get in the back seat of the big blue car. The plastic-covered seats stick to my legs, which dangle over the edge. I look out of the window at the sky. Aunt Merleen drives like police are chasing her. Aunt Faith gives a little grunt every time we go through a red light. Aunt Merleen wheels sharply into the gravel parking lot of Macedonia First Baptist, a simple red brick building surrounded by shade trees on one side and the highway on the other. I cry out as I bounce off the back seat onto the floor.

"Baby, you all right?" Aunt Faith asks me. I nod yes, but I know Aunt Merleen did it on purpose.

"Maybe your aunt Faith will teach you how to drive once she learns herself," Aunt Merleen says. Aunt Faith straightens her hat and pretends she hasn't heard that comment before we walk through the double doors of the church with her holding my hand. They don't seem to realize I won't be here long enough for them to teach me much.

I have never seen the inside of a church. My eyes record this new place like a camera. We step into a dark little foyer with a sweaty water fountain on the right wall and a window on the other where Aunt Faith stops to pay her church dues. We stand waiting in front of another set of double doors. I hear the sound of muffled pleas. Suddenly I hear singing that seems to rise up from a deep, rich, fertile place and music so lively I want to dance. The music pulls on me, the singing grabs me by the arms and shakes me. So I move, trying to get out of the way. I start shuffling my feet and moving my hips until Aunt Merleen snatches me by my frilly collar and whispers into my ear, "No finger popping in here." My heart is beating in my ears as two sets of white-gloved hands push open the doors to let us in. A man in a suit and a woman in a white uniform like Mama's are smiling down at me. Everybody in the church stands up. My nervous legs follow the blood-red carpet to the front of the church. We walk between rows of wooden benches filled with powdered, perfumed, dressed-up older women wearing elaborate hats and young girls with shiny pressed hair rocking crying babies. The few men there are standing along the wall with a white-gloved hand across their chest or sitting in what I learn is the amen corner in the front of the church on the right. The amen corner on the left is filled with the mothers of the church—old women with white handkerchiefs on their head. We sit in the third row from the front every Sunday from then on. On Easter Sunday or Mother's Day when it is overcrowded I sit on Aunt Faith's lap. My first Sunday in church is not unpleasant. I watch the light burn through the stained-glass windows onto the blood-red carpet.

The singing is nice and when the preacher becomes long-winded I fall asleep and drool into the lap of Aunt Faith's dress until I wake up to the sound of somebody getting happy. One of the mothers of the church is filled with the spirit. The old woman, with eyes closed, leaps from her seat and jumps in place as she testifies and says amens all over the place.

"What wrong with that lady?" I lean in, whispering to Aunt Faith.

"Sister Rose is happy. She's shouting so God can hear her," Aunt Faith whispers back, patting me on the hand as if to soothe me. The mother of the church is joined in spirit catching by a number of other ladies every Sunday. If one of them faints, an usher in white will run a bottle of smelling salts under her nose and the men will help her to a room in the back of the church where someone will fan her until she is free of the spirit. I decide to shout myself one Sunday. I simply shout to God the thing I want the most: "Mama. Mama. Mama. Amen." Then I sit down and fall asleep again.

After church the right hand of fellowship is offered. Everybody shakes hands with everybody else as we leave the church. Young women pinch my cheeks and say how cute I look. Old ladies ooh and aah over me, patting me on my head and whispering words like *shame* and *pitiful.* I walk over to sit in the shade of a thick-branched tree watching the old ladies looking at me and shaking their heads at whatever Aunt Merleen is saying to them under the chinaberry tree across the parking lot. A girl older than me, wearing a dark green coat dress that is too big for her, comes over to where I am digging in the dirt with a stick. Her short shiny curls frame her head like a crown. She smiles and a gold tooth flashes left of center in her mouth. She seems too happy to keep it to herself.

"You've got the prettiest eyes. I'll bet you've got a pretty smile too," she says, sitting down on the thick tree root beside me.

"My name is Joanne. Do you want to go to the Candy Man's house with me?" Her big round eyes are a strange caramel color and her lashes are thick and long. I like the way she smells like a flower that bees dream about when their honey is gone. Not waiting for an answer she takes my hand and we stand up together. I wish she was my mama, that I could go home with her.

"Your auntie said it was okay for you come with me. It ain't far." She sounds like my mama did when we rolled into Georgia, sweet and childlike with a way of talking that softens words in her mouth, makes them strange yet soothing. I look over to where my aunts are talking and Aunt Merleen waves us on. I turn and follow Joanne down a rocky dirt path to the back door of a wooden shotgun house a few yards from the church. Joanne talks and I listen. She tells me that she lives down the street from my aunts with her mother who smokes too much and her grandmother who writes letters to dead people and watches tv all day and curses at the mailman if he doesn't bring her anything but bills. "I've got a boyfriend but my mama's so strict she'll only let me see him at church and Henry ain't hardly the church-going type," she says laughing.

Joanne knocks on the old screen door twice. An old man in a wheel-chair rolls up to it. Patches of white hair sprout on his head and on his dark brown gaunt cheeks. A wide wooden box filled with different kinds of candies is laid across the lap of his baggy green military pants.

"Good afternoon," Joanne says. "Two coconuts please." The Candy Man pushes open the screen and hands Joanne two red, white, and yellow striped coconut bars. She pays him with a crisp one-dollar bill. Without a word he gives her change from the breast pocket of his dirty white tee shirt.

"Thank you and God bless," Joanne says as we carefully walk down the steps.

"He don't talk. He was wounded in the war or something. I tried to interview him for a project at school one time but he don't never talk. He'll take your money though."

We walk slowly toward the parking lot where Aunt Merleen and Aunt Faith are sitting in the big blue car waiting for us. Before we get close where they can hear us Joanne stops walking and looks down at me with the kindest face.

"Do you know how to dance?" she asks me.

I shake my head no.

"Don't be so sad," she says, snapping her teeth on the coconut candy. "If you stop tying up your face I'll ask your aunts if you can come over to my house and I'll show you how."

"Thank you," I say, swallowing the sticky sweet candy. I am grateful for her small kindness, sure she will save me from my aunts, but I never see her again. Aunt Faith says she ran off to live with her boyfriend, a soldier stationed somewhere in Florida. I am beginning to see that nothing lasts long, not even hope.

*E*very Sunday after church we go to see my grandmother at the Resurrection Rest Home. The smell of ammonia is strong coming down the long bright fluorescent hall lined with old people tied to wheelchairs. Grandmother Gert cries when she sees us. Her grief is short.

"What you bring me?" My grandmother's thin dry fingers pick at the plate of food like claws. She wrinkles up her broad nose in anticipation.

"I hope you didn't bring me no more of that ash-dry cornbread. I want some oxtail soup like Mama used to make. Some meaty tails with a thick gravy and some long grain rice on the side." She uncovers the aluminum foil and once her disappointment is confirmed she pushes the plate aside and folds her hands in her lap.

"I gave that lap quilt you give me to a lady down the hall. She ain't got no family so I give her that quilt. Your stitches still uneven and bumpy. That cheap yarn you use makes me itch." She scratches her ashy arms as if remembering the feel of it on her skin. I step back behind Aunt Faith and try to lose my sense of hearing and my sense of smell. I try to make myself disappear, but nothing works.

"They had to tie down poor Mrs. Donnell but she's all right now. She didn't want to take no more medicine. Say it make her sleep all the time. She might as well be dead much as she sleep. Them nurses want to keep us drugged like addicts. Faith, you big as a house. How you think you gonna get a husband big as you are? Mama's people were big. Aunt Dot weighed about three hundred pounds, didn't she?" She doesn't let up on her one-way conversation, taking stabs at Aunt Merleen and Aunt Faith as if they were Christmas dinner.

My grandmother complains about her aches and pains, how bad the food is, how wicked the nurses are. She never speaks to me and doesn't seem to notice that I am in the room. I hate her from the moment she opens her mouth, twisted north and south by a stroke. She looks dry and empty and smells like urine and dust. Aunt Faith pushes the wobbly wheelchair into the garden where we sit with other visiting families, not saying much for the next hour. Speaking quickly and loudly, Gert comments on how much gray hair her sisters have. She takes particular pleasure in asking if Faith is pregnant yet. After she laughs at them and calls them "sister" like it was a bad word, she cries and begs them to take her home, saying she could clean house and make good cornbread. She never asks about my mama.

"I know sex secrets. I'll tell you how to get a man and keep him if you take me home," she says in a loud whisper, smiling her crooked smile.

In the car on the way to the big white house Aunt Faith cries. Later Aunt Merleen is even more cold and distant, gardening in the dark. I lie in my bed feeling sorry for my mother. If I'd had a mother like mean, smelly old Gert Rainey, I would've run away and made a baby to love me too. I am hungry for a mother's love. I keep waiting for words to grow in the garden of my heart, magic words to bring my mama back.

# THREE

*I* set the bed on fire, then stand in the doorway watching it burn. The flame from the first match flickered, then died. The second match caught, then blazed before my eyes. I stare into the flames and see my mother's hands reaching out to me, the treacherous lump thickening in my throat as I reach for her. I've set the bed on fire. The bed where I dream Mama's dreams and sweat through her nightmares, running from her enemies. I stand in the doorway watching it burn. I miss my mama, but I don't want to. I am seven years old and yesterday is today, tomorrow never comes.

Pushing me aside Aunt Merleen grabs the white enamel pitcher of water that always sits on my bedside table. She dashes out the fire.

I hear Aunt Faith singing, "My bed. My beautiful bed." Sweet soprano.

Aunt Merleen just shakes her head to the tune of "Umph, umph, umph." Rumbling bass.

The smoke fills my ears and coats my tongue with sadness. The burning dreams fill up my lungs with longing.

"Is she dead?" I ask from the doorway, looking at Aunt Faith's tiny bare feet.

"No child, she's not dead," Aunt Faith answers sadly.

Her answer smashes all hope against the wall. If she were dead I could stop waiting. If she were dead I could die too.

"Why did she leave me?" I scream at them and bang my head against the doorframe over and over until Aunt Faith draws me up to her, holding my head against her belly. She lets me cry and scream for days into her soft, smoky apron. I don't ask about Mama again for a long time. I begin sleeping on a quilt on the hardwood floor that smells of lemon oil. I stop dreaming and begin to see shadows underneath the bed.

One Sunday after visiting Grandma Gert, Aunt Faith tells Aunt Merleen to drop her off at the hospital to visit one of the sick members of the church. I am left alone with the stormy one. I follow her in through the back door of the house. I take off my shiny black church shoes and put them in their box by the back door. I put on the pink ballet slippers they have asked me to wear in the house. Then I drag the stepstool over to the kitchen sink where I scrub my hands with Ivory liquid dish soap and a rough bristled brush just like they have taught me. I walk down the narrow carpeted hallway lined with framed poems and prayers and sit on the bottom step of the front stairs looking at the closed front door as if it will fly open and my mama will be standing there with her hands on her hips ready to take me away. I can almost see her soft, smooth hand beckoning me to her. That is what I pray for every Sunday, so I sit and wait and hope. Aunt Merleen ignores me mostly. When I hear her grumbling, something about the bed, I try not to, but I cry.

"You miss her, don't you?" Her voice is a thunderous whisper beside me.

I can't speak, but nod my head yes, wiping the tears away.

"Come on." Her bark is softer as she turns to walk away.

I look up to make sure she is speaking to me.

"Come on. I won't bite you." She is smiling a little.

I follow her into the kitchen. She hands me a pair of stiff blue overalls, a blue flannel boy's shirt, and a pair of black high-top sneakers. I drop the yellow girly Sunday dress to the slick linoleum floor and slip into a boy's world. Spring into summer, I get my hands dirty oiling screws from the lawn mower and planting rosebushes. My fingers become bloody from carving wooden birds and fish. I run. I climb trees. I throw rocks at tin cans. I am distracted from the pain that makes me want to set myself on fire. For many nights I sleep in my new boy's clothes, dreaming about my new life.

Aunt Merleen is hard on the outside, but I learn where she keeps her softness. She can't stand to see pain the way some people can't stand to see blood. I keep her secrets and she keeps mine.

Because she thinks most of the neighborhood children are thieves and future criminals she won't let me play with them. It is too far to play with the children I meet in Sunday school so I play alone, games

I remember and ones I make up to pass the time. I read the books Aunt Faith buys for me and act out stories in front of the mirror. I am Cleopatra, Delilah, Mary Magdalen, and the Queen of Sheba, one after the other and all at once. I am also Harriet Tubman on the Underground Railroad and Frederick Douglass giving a speech, Mighty Mouse and Batman.

Across the railroad tracks are the government housing projects. From my bedroom window I watch the project children jump rope, play hopscotch in the dirt and dodge ball, and skate on the broken sidewalks. I imagine myself in their games, but I end up playing all by myself. All summer long I pretend that I am a boy, doing boy things, wearing boy clothes.

*S*chool breaks our routine. On my first day at the red brick school down the street, I insist on wearing my boy's clothes.

"Little girls just don't wear pants to school," Aunt Faith says patiently, waiting for me to change my mind.

"Aunt Merleen wears pants all the time," I say, hooking my thumbs firmly in the shoulder straps of my overalls just as I have seen Aunt Merleen do when taking a break in her garden to consider the flowers, fruits, and vegetables of her labor.

"That's different. These are my work clothes. If I were going to school I'd wear school clothes." Aunt Merleen is taking her time with me and I can tell she is getting weak because she starts pacing back and forth outside my bedroom in the hallway, trying to think up a good argument. I'd figured out how to soften them up so I could get my way. They hardly ever said no to anything I asked for. Pretty soon I figured I'd be driving the car to meet my mama at the train station.

"Pretty please?" I say, giving them the most pitiful look I can manage.

They both laugh and throw up their hands as if I have won this round.

"You've got your mama's ways. Get your sweater and your book satchel and let's go before you completely miss your first day at school," Aunt Merleen says as she walks heavily down the stairs. She is wearing a plain plaid shift dress I've never seen her wear before and a pair of run-over loafers she wears when she works in the garden. She drives me down the street to the school and walks me up to the door.

"Mind the teacher and do your best," she says, and opens the door to my classroom. She waves at the teacher from the top of the stairs and lets go of my hand. I look at the rows of solemn faces looking back at me. Only one face is smiling, a girl with a limp pink ribbon in her hair. By the time I look back Aunt Merleen is gone. From the moment I descend the stairs into the large basement classroom the teacher refuses to teach me, the children tease me and refuse to play with me because I am different. None of the other girls wear pants. They are all frilly girly-girls all tied up with satin ribbons. They call me names and throw rocks at me. I play alone on the monkey bars, making up words to songs. I want to cry, but I don't. The next day I wear one of the dresses Aunt Faith has remade for me, a navy blue sailor dress with white buttons that float down the front. The dress reminds me of my mama.

I make friends with a girly-girl who wears flowered dresses and pale pink ragged ribbons in her long dark hair. She is a project girl. Her name is Joyous, but I call her Joy because she is always giggling even when there is nothing to laugh at. She is tongue tied so she calls me Myra. I like the way she says it. In her mouth my name is an unexpected happiness. We become so close that when we come to a pole or a tree or an old tire in the road we always hold hands and step around it together, on the same side. We know that it is bad luck to split a pole. You always follow the person you love when you come to an obstacle in the road. She comes with me to the big white house. I can tell that Aunt Merleen does not approve, but she doesn't say any-thing, not even good evening. Aunt Faith is nicer, she gives us a plate of cookies dusted with powdered sugar and short glasses of milk. I have to show Joy where to put her shoes and how to put the pink bal-let shoes over her socks and scrub her hands in the sink until they are clean.

We play on the screened-in side porch which looks out onto the garden. Joy tells me she is part Indian. I wonder which part. I tell her that makes us sisters because my mama is part Cherokee. I tell her that there is some Spanish in my blood too. To prove it, I teach her some of the words my mother gave me.

*Bonita . . . encaje . . . dulce . . . azul . . . música . . . sueño . . .*

We make dolls out of Aunt Faith's French magazines, Coke bot-tles, broken shoe strings, buttons, and glue. We fill the bottles with sweet lemonade and color it with dye and drink it till our lips are the color of blue roses and just as soft when she teaches me how to kiss. And we kiss for hours, years go by and our lips and our eyes remain closed, together. We discover other secret feelings in my bedroom with the door closed. I like touching her closed eyes with my lips, pressing my tongue in her belly button, brushing against her soft, fat thighs with my cheeks. I hide crayons and nervous fingers between her legs to see how far they will go. We hide under the bed playing house, in the closet playing doctor. When we play Beach Blanket Bingo under blankets thrown over chairs I am Frankie and she is Annette. I am al-ways in charge.

Even though she lives across the railroad tracks in a tiny cement block apartment facing an alley, across the street from a cemetery and around the corner from the projects, Joy is still a project girl. She says that when it rains they have to put pots and pans on the floor to catch the leaks in the ceiling. She lives in a three-room apartment with her mother, Nag, her stepfather, Jack, two sisters, and brother. She and her older sister Nicky sleep on a big lumpy bed in the bedroom, her brother Lark sleeps on a cot next to the stove in the kitchen. Her mother and stepfather and the new baby, Erica, named after a soap-opera star, sleep on a fold-out couch in the living room. It is so different from the house where I live. The house where I live has a place for everything. Everything in its place. It smells like fresh flowers and lemon oil and Aunt Faith's musty sweetness. The apartment where Joy lives is rich with the smell of fried foods, used baby diapers, and the Lucky Strike cigarettes her mother smokes constantly. Sometimes I wish Joy could live with us. There is enough room for her whole family in the big white house with room left over, but somehow I don't think Aunt Faith or Aunt Merleen would see it that way. Her mother tells me to call her Nag.

One day me and Joy are caught kissing. Her mother catches us and I become a girl again as if I have been a butterfly that becomes a rock.

"It's an abomination before God," her mother declares and makes us pray together on our knees on the dirty kitchen floor. Baby Erica's crying competes with the tv on full volume from the next room and mixes with our loud prayers for forgiveness. Her mother chants scriptures into the sticky air for hours. Then she walks me home. She walks three steps ahead of me wearing a sleeveless faded green shift that once zipped up the front but is now held together in two places with huge silver safety pins. Her blue flip flops sound like wet hands slapping the pavement. The night claws at me, closing me in. Joy's mother walks me right up to the door of the big white house. I am so scared I start to cry before Nag can speak. But she speaks. She tells everything she knows and my future if I do not change my wicked ways. Aunt Merleen listens to Nag through the screen door. She tells me to come in the house, but does not invite Nag beyond the top step of the porch.

"You won't have to worry about her no more. She's not allowed down in the projects no way. Thank you for bringing her home. Good night, *Miss* Dyson." Aunt Merleen closes the door in her face. I can still hear Nag cursing us out on the porch in the dark.

"You late for supper," Aunt Merleen says, taking long strides down the hall to the kitchen. I follow her, wondering what she is going to do to me. She chooses each sentence carefully. "Your aunt Faith is at choir rehearsal. She don't need to know about all this." She pauses, bites her lip, then says: "I told you not to play with them project children."

Aunt Merleen starts talking to the can of soup she is opening for my supper. "You ought to wait until you a little bit older to go around kissing. Kissing and all that is for grown folks." And that is the last word she says on the subject. A secret we keep from Aunt Faith. I spend hours in my room thinking of the day when I am older, when I am a butterfly and can start kissing girls again.

Me and the girly-girl are friends for a long time after this, but we never kiss on the lips again or find secret places to play on each other's bodies. We don't speak of those times, but I never forget them. I can't stop thinking about kissing. My friend the girly-girl encourages me to wear dresses. I look like I fit in, but I never do.

"Where is my mama's suitcase?" I ask when I miss Mama so much my chest hurts from the pain. The two years I've waited for her seem like an unfair prison sentence. I am nine years old and I feel that I have been very patient, but I have also grown curious. Answers to my questions are as scarce as answered prayers.

"We put it up for her," Aunt Faith says without looking up from her sewing.

"Could I see it? Maybe she left her address in there." I sit next to the piano unraveling a thread at the bottom of my shirt.

"Your mama don't have an address, baby. She's traveling."

"You heard from my mama?" I ask, wide-eyed. "When she coming to get me?"

"We didn't exactly hear from her," Aunt Faith says quietly.

"Reverend Wilson's son-in-law saw her in Atlanta last year. She said she'd send for you as soon as she could," Aunt Merleen says flatly from her chair, exchanging a look with Aunt Faith that says more than my ears will hear. She makes a great noise of turning the pages of the newspaper stretched out in front of her.

"What's she doing in Atlanta?" I keep picking at the threads. They fall on the carpet making patterns like a cat's cradle.

"She was working, getting ready to go to Memphis, I think he said." Aunt Faith keeps moving the needle and thread in tight tiny stitches that will be invisible to the eye.

"She'll come back to get you when she can. In the meantime, ain't we doing all right? Why don't you read me one of them Simple stories by Langston Hughes. He write some funny stories, don't he?" Aunt Merleen quickly folds up her newspaper and talks fast like she is trying to hurry Mama out of my mind, but I'm not having it.

"Didn't she leave a address? I could write to her at the post office in Memphis. She probably waiting on a letter from me. Can I look in her suitcase?"

"There ain't nothing in that suitcase concern you. It's for your mama when she come back. Now leave it alone." Aunt Merleen's tone hits me in the stomach. I pick up the broken threads from the carpet and take them with me to my room to poke into the windowscreen like constellations in the sky. I refuse to let them see me cry.

I want to look for the suitcase but I am never left alone in the house. I suspect they keep it in their bedroom which I have only seen from the doorway next to the bathroom. It is a large room with neat twin beds made up with colorful patterned quilts. The beds are separated by a small night table. There is also a dark wood vanity beneath a smoky mirror, a matching chifforobe with a place for Aunt Faith's Sunday hats, and a tall chest of drawers. Aunt Merleen's shotgun lies like a sleeping soldier under her bed. Everything is in its place. A place for everything, but me. I am on the outside with my nose pressed to the window waiting for something that is mine.

*I*ndian summers and dog days go by. Holidays and birthdays pass as quietly as grass grows. Not one word from her. I am so mad at my mama for leaving me I am not sure I can forgive her. Life is so difficult without her. At the Parent & Teachers' Association meetings I am stuck sitting with Aunt Faith, who my teacher thinks is my grandmother. At church on Mother's Day Aunt Faith and Aunt Merleen wear white flowers pinned to their dresses because their mother is dead. I am forced to wear a red flower because my mother is alive, but I feel as if she is dead. I wish I could wear a pink satin rose for my mother because she is missing.

In school the other children tease me.

"Where's your mama?" they ask, as if they are interested.

Not waiting for an answer, some of them speculate.

"Maybe she's in jail." Everybody laughs, everybody but Dwight James, whose mama is in prison for killing his daddy because he beat her one time too many.

"Or at the welfare office trying to get some government cheeeeese." Their laughter is like a cloud of bees stinging me from all sides.

Before I can think of something smart to say back, another girl says, "I bet she ain't even got no mama." I learn to pretend that I am deaf to their insults. In two blinks I can grow cement in my ears. If I focus on the color blue I can sometimes hear music in my head . . . *sweet* . . . *blue* . . . *music* . . . The sky is all I need, or a page in a book or the hem of a skirt as long as it is blue.

During library period, I excuse myself to go to the bathroom. The librarian, Miss Belton, is a graceful middle-aged woman who wears her hair in two thick black braids wrapped like coiled snakes on top of her head. She likes me, so I don't have to beg like some of the other students. She waves me out of the room, her hand caressing the air as delicate as a lady's handkerchief. The long wide hallway echoes with the sound of my footsteps. Two flights down in the basement, the girls' bathroom is one big open room with a row of white porcelain toilets facing a row of white sinks and squares of chrome-framed mirrors. I am washing my hands in the sink. When I look up I see two upper-class girls come in. Sonya is the baddest girl in school. She is the biggest too. She has stayed back twice in the fourth grade. I think this is what has made her so mean. Her shadow Victoria is with her. Victoria does everything Sonya tells her. They beat up a girl after school one time and took her lunch money every day for a month before the girl's mama told the principal. Sonya got sent home for a week. She came back with a broken arm somebody said her brother gave her and she was meaner than ever. When they see me they start laughing. I keep lathering my hands with the smooth bar of orange soap that smells like medicine. Sonya starts in on me.

"Look at her, looking in the mirror like she something." Her voice is rough and accusing.

Then Victoria gives me a shot. "Think you something don't you? Think you cute."

"And with a stupid name like Mariah Santos you must be Mexican or something."

"You Mexican Sand Toes? Is that why you think you so good?"

I blink twice but I am so mad I can hear them through the cement in my ears. I look around but I can't find the color blue. Even the sky is gray. I don't know what to say. Victoria pushes me against the sink. I am about to throw soap in her eyes when Joy comes in. Her skirt circles the air as she whirls around and stands in between them and me with both hands on her hips like she is Marshall Dillon on "Gunsmoke." Like a hired assasin on "The Wild, Wild West."

"You messing with my friend?" she says, puffing up like she's six feet tall instead of five feet even.

"What's it to you?" Sonya asks, taking a step forward.

"If you messing with my friend, you messing with me, and if you mess with me, my sister Nicky will kick your ass." Joy tosses her hair over her shoulder and stands her ground. Still life in motion. Sonya is the one to back down. Nicky is always in trouble for fighting at the junior high school and rumor has it she bit a girl so hard you can still see the teeth marks on her face.

"Ain't nobody messing with you or your stuck-up little friend. Come on, Vic, let's go. It stinks in here," Sonya says, dismissing us with a wave of her hand as she leaves the bathroom.

When they leave I breathe again and let go of the sink. I am relieved I didn't have to fight the biggest girl in the school. I don't even know how to fight. No one has taught me how. Until then I'd never needed to defend myself with anything other than words. I don't know what to say. I want to kiss her, but the girly-girl steps away from me.

"I can't do that anymore. I'll get in trouble. My mama says we'll go to hell in a handbasket." She leans back against the sink and smiles.

"I'm sorry. I don't want you to go to hell." I stand awkwardly in the middle of the room, chewing on the side of my finger, not caring whether I go to hell or not.

"It's okay. You're still my friend to the end. You my girl, but you can't let people walk over you. I'm not always gonna come like Batman right on time to save your ass. If anybody mess with you, you pick up a brick or a rock or the biggest thing you can find and before they can blink, you knock the hell out of the biggest one in the bunch and they'll leave you alone." She shows me how to use an empty Coke bottle as a weapon. Before we leave the bathroom she winks at me. I wink back just like she taught me two summers past.

When a girl twice my size says, "Hey Santos, I saw your mama down on Eighth Street turning tricks at the gas station," I say, "You say that when I get back." I go back into the big white house and fill a Coke bottle with water. I drop a broken Alka-Seltzer in the water and watch it fizz. I go back outside and I yell at her, "Come over here and say that to my face. I'll burn your ass with this acid. I'll put your lights out." I throw the bottle at her. It sails through the air and lands a few feet from her dirty tennis shoes. She runs off yelling, "You crazy, Santos. You crazy. They ought to send you to Milledgeville." Nobody messed with me after that. I was left alone. Word got around fast: "Crazy Santos. The girl is mad."

My teachers at school reward my good behavior and excellent memory with straight A's and I continue to set an example for the other students, which does not earn me many friends outside of class. Miss Belton lets me check out books on Mexico. I know I'm not supposed to deface a library book, but I cut out one of the colored maps so that I can sleep with it under my pillow. I dream of a different Mexican city and village each night and in these dreams I walk the streets and dusty unpaved roads looking for my father, hoping he has found my mother and that they are waiting for me to join them so that together we can paint the sky blue.

I miss my friend the girly-girl. Her easy giggles and house games. Neicey only plays with me because my aunt gives her piano lessons and she has to wait for her father to pick her up in his taxi. We don't talk much. She is really stuck up. She lives in a house in Randall Estates and goes to Catholic school even though her family is Baptist. After her Saturday morning lessons we play Candyland, Monopoly, or checkers until she hears her father ringing the doorbell. She doesn't even bother to say good-bye when he comes, just smoothes down the folds of her velvet dress as if she has gotten dirty playing with me. My aunts think she is sweet, but a girl who cheats at checkers is low class, I don't care where she goes to school.

# FOUR

"We're not really sisters," Aunt Merleen says casually one Sunday evening as we sit on the back porch carving owls from blocks of fragrant hardwood. Out of the corner of my eye I watch her and wait. I keep my head down just like she does, concentrating on the outstretched wings of the owl.

"We're kin though, cousins. Our fathers were brothers. They worked on the railroad together. We lived next door to each other from the time we were born."

My knife slips and nicks my thumb. I stick my finger in my mouth and suck on it.

"We still kin to Gert? Is she still my grandmother?" I didn't like that mean old woman and never would. I hoped I had none of her blood in me.

"She's Faith's sister in truth. You getting big now. I told Faith it's time you learned some things about the family." She hesitates, looking over at me to see just how much she can tell. At ten I am big for my age. I have outgrown two pairs of overalls and my favorite cowboy shirt. Aunt Merleen turns her eyes to the owl and begins to tell it everything. Almost everything.

"Faith and me, we always been best friends. Gert's the one tried to run a stake through our friendship. She always been jealous of Faith's pretty. The boys always wanted to talk to Faith no matter who else was around. Pretty inside and out. One Easter Gert stole some matches and unfiltered cigarettes and made us watch her play like she was a movie star. We was teenagers, but we knew our folks would skin us alive for smoking stolen cigarettes. We heard somebody coming and Gert threw the lit cigarette under the bed. It caught on some newspapers and the flames ate up the curtains Faith was hiding behind. Faith lit up like a Christmas tree. She screamed and cried, but Gert just looked at her from the door and ran out of the room laughing. I threw a quilt over her and I don't know how, but I dragged her out of the house. We all got out alive, but their house burned to the ground, left nothing but the chimney and a handful of ashes. Their family moved in with mine. We been sisters ever since.

"I don't know how the flames didn't scar up her face or her hands or her feet, but they didn't. She looks all right on the outside, but that brave little woman lives in pain. Because of all that, being disfigured like she was, she didn't think she'd ever get married; I knew I wouldn't. We've lived together forty-seven years. Sometimes I love Faith like a sister, most times . . . most times I just love her."

Tears seem to well up, then retreat in her eyes. She folds up her knife and puts the rest of the story away.

After Aunt Merleen tells me this story we seem to understand one another. It is clear we both know something about the relationship between love and pain. She secretly begins to teach me how to drive. I am a fast learner. Driving takes my mind off Mama for a while. I pretend that I will be waiting for her at the train station when her train comes this way again. I'm sure it will and I'll be there waiting.

*A*unt Faith is a tireless teacher. Even when I am tuneless and irritable she waits for my mood to pass before continuing the lesson. We sometimes sit in a puddle of thick silence on the bench in the music room after I have made one mistake after another.

"Mariah, you are trying my patience today." I often hate her for trying to be my mama, but today, especially. I make mistakes on purpose to irritate her. By the way she is breathing I know that she is counting to twenty. We sit quietly in the room with the shutters closed against the summer light. I am feeling mean and though I think I know the whole answer to the question, I ask it anyway.

"How come you never got married and had your own children?" I ask, lacing my fingers together in my lap.

She lets the yellow ruler she uses to mark time drop to the carpet, then follows the sound of my voice. Her eyes lock with mine, then become sad and far away.

"I was seventeen once. My face was young and pretty and I filled my favorite lavender summer dress with a shapely figure. I laughed all the time and played the piano just because it gave me pleasure. I met

Lincoln in a French class taught by an old Creole lady from New Orleans just before he was drafted. He played that cello over there."

She points to a tall, dark case shaped like a woman leaning against the wall listening to us.

"He had the soul of a poet. He could find music in almost any sound. He was always humming, tapping his fingers against tabletops and writing the most soulful songs. Lincoln had a great love of music and poetry. He was such a sensitive man. I've often wondered what my life would have been like if he had come back or if we had found him. After the war he wrote me a letter from France."

Aunt Faith pulls a fragile leaf of stationery from between the pages of her hymn book and reads aloud to me.

*Faith my treasure,*

*I have decided to continue my studies here in France and have formed a trio. I am remaining in this haven, because it is safe to be an intelligent, educated Negro here. I have yet to be called a nigger or treated like one. You my dear would do well to consider a life of freedom in this foreign land. I hope to see you again someday. I miss the tenderness of your sweet southern charm.*

*Sincerely yours,*

*Lincoln A. Porter.*

"We heard he married a white woman and that they moved to Switzerland. I couldn't believe that, though. Not the way he hated white people. She might've been light skinned. He liked slender girls with light skin and long hair, said they would make pretty babies."

I try hard to imagine Aunt Faith pretty and slender in a lavender summer dress. I wonder if she thinks my nut brown skin and nappy hair are pretty.

"He himself was pecan colored with thick, wavy hair. Don't tell Merleen I told you about Lincoln, it always makes her sad. We had a habit of loving the same things."

She pauses to show me a photograph of a smiling young man posing with his arm around the neck of a cello.

"We would've made such pretty babies, but Merleen said he was too handsome to be a husband."

I think I have won because I made her cry, but she simply continues my lesson with the same fierce determination to civilize me with music.

*I* open the dusty case and stroke the polished, golden veneer of wood, caressing the curves and plucking the strings. I find the bow and lift the cello from its home. I have never seen anything more beautiful. I want it desperately. I hold it close to my heart and I pray. Aunt Faith lets me keep the cello in my room where I polish it every day.

When I am older Aunt Faith hires Mr. Giovanni to give me lessons. Mr. Giovanni is an elegant old man who wears bow ties with dark, shiny suits, and smells like sour cheese. He is an Italian Jew from New Jersey. An old professor from the music school where Aunt Faith studied. He sits close to me with his eyes closed, swaying to some other music while I play. He makes noises in his throat when he is pleased, clucks his tongue when he is not. He is not often pleased with my playing. My fingers are clumsy and I am impatient. I want to sound like the music on the radio, sweet, soulful, and sad. My playing sounds like I am dropping stones in the mud.

"You seem like such a sad little girl. What do you have to be so sad about?"

I am shy with him so I say nothing. I have no words to speak of the deep loneliness I feel. He does not press. Sometimes after a lesson Mr. Giovanni tells me fairy tales. The sound of his voice is like music. I close my eyes to listen to the crunch of bones as disobedient children are eaten by German ogres, or the hissing of a giant snake about to crush an egg thief in India or the cackling of evil old women who turn bad little girls into logs and toss them on the fire to warm themselves.

"Do you have a little girl?" I ask, wondering if he tells these stories to other children.

"How old are you?" he answers with a question.

"Eleven."

"My Anna's birthday is next week. She played the violin."

"Is she pretty?" I am jealous.

"She was. She played like Paganini, but better."

This prompts Mr. Giovanni to tell me the story of his life. It is sad and full of loss and regrets. Most of his family was murdered during the war.

"Giuditta, Uncle Pepi, Benjamino, Anna. All gone," he says.

He remembers the color of their eyes, the shape of their hands, the sound of their happiness. He has numbers tattooed on his arm and deep private scars no one can see. I have seen pictures of the war and I have read stories. I can tell he leaves out the sound of crushing bones, the smell of burning flesh, and the sight of delicate flakes of human ashes in dark gray skies. For many years he said he did not want to live but he had to tell the story and he had music to play.

"If you are going to live, then do not starve yourself or others," he tells me with the voice of experience, patting me on my shoulder awkwardly.

I do not starve myself. I eat plenty. I am trying to fill the hole left by Mama. But everything I used to cry over seems small after Mr. Giovanni tells me his story. Everything, but missing Mama.

Aunt Merleen says Jew Baby is as pretty as a girl. His real name is Samson, but everybody calls him Jew Baby because he was born in Germany and because when he talks he sounds like his tongue is cut in half. One time when Mr. Giovanni is giving me a cello lesson Jew Baby comes early for a piano lesson. He sticks his head in the room and starts making faces at me. He starts swaying to the music just like Mr. Giovanni. I get mad because I think he is making fun of Mr. Giovanni.

"Jew Baby, stop. That ain't funny," I say, throwing my fist at him. He runs off toward the kitchen screaming like a thief.

"What did you call him?" Mr. Giovanni asks, turning to face me.

"Jew Baby. That's his play name." I rub the bow across an itchy mosquito bite on my ankle.

"Why do you call him that?"

"Because he talks funny. He was born overseas, in Germany."

Mr. Giovanni looks at me with the saddest eyes. "The Germans called us names and killed Jews because we were different. Because you speak well, it does not give you the right to make fun of him. Do you see? I am a Jew and it is a good thing. You are colored and that is just as good."

"I'm sorry. I didn't mean nothing. Everybody calls him that." I twist uncomfortably under his gaze.

"Don't be a follower," he says, and I look at the numbers on his arm. Mr. Giovanni tells me another one of his fairy tales and then he gives me a little blue wooden spinning top. I never call Samson out of his name again and pretty soon he is talking just like the rest of us colored people living in Georgia, losing the end of words and making up other ones.

Soon after Mr. Giovanni takes me to a classical music concert at the newly integrated auditorium, he stops giving me cello lessons. Aunt Faith tells me he has died in his sleep. I am not sad. I know that he is telling fairy tales to his daughter in heaven.

Without lessons I play the cello finding sounds of my own. I slap her right breast, beating her like a drum as if I am in a trance. I improvise according to my moods, moving my fingers up and down the strings along her neck and drawing the bow across the hollow of her waist for hours. At first it sounds as if I am sawing wood but then I begin to feel the music in my bones. Sometimes I can make the cello sing. Sometimes I make her cry. My cello makes the most beautiful sounds. I name her Rosemary. She becomes my best friend. Sometimes I fall asleep with her in my arms.

*My head sits on top of Rosemary's body. I am wearing a bow tie like Mr. Giovanni's. My legs dangle just beneath her hips. My feet are bare and tattooed with blue numbers. My arms are joined to the wood beside her waist. We are transformed into one thing, inseparable. My left hand plucks a lullaby, fingers pinching the strings until they moan, the other hand slides up and down our body until we are dripping wet. Making love with Rosemary is like making love with myself, delicious and forbidden.*

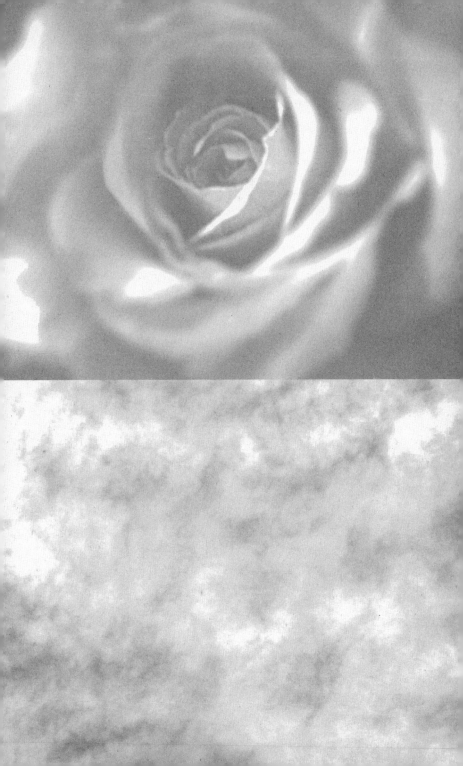

FIVE

$\mathcal{I}$'m not exactly sure what it is I am looking for. At first I am nervous my aunts will catch me rambling through their things, but when I find my treasure, I don't care. I have not seen the green suitcase since I arrived in this house. Since the day Mama left me with them. I find it hidden in back of Aunt Faith's

locked chifforobe, underneath several boxes of shoes. The keys to all
the locked places have been left on the kitchen table. They have gone
to church without me. I told them I was sick, throwing up on the
kitchen floor to make a stronger case for staying home. I am sick, sick
of going to church every Sunday. Sick of my mean old grandmother
Gert treating me like a roach she refuses to see on our visits to her in
the nursing home.

The first pale blue page in Mama's diary reads, *Curiosity killed the cat,
but satisfaction brought him back. Matisse stained me with passion.* From January
second to September fifteenth the pages are torn out. The next entry
is on my birthday, September twenty-second. Here Mama has writ-
ten, *I cried like hell, but there's an angel in my arms tonight.* The rest of the
pages are blank. I taste each word she has written, savoring the memory of their sweet pain. I read between each blank line searching for
her fingerprints, a tear, her breath, one drop of blood.

I sit on the floor of my aunt's room. I unfold two pink satin slips,
a black garter, a pair of black stockings, and a blurry photograph of
me and Mama lying on the bed we used to share. Her arm is around
me. Her legs are bare, crossed at the thigh. She is wearing a satin slip.
She is smiling, looking directly into the camera with a whiskey glass
raised in a toast. I remember lying on the itchy, dark wool blanket. I
remember it all so clearly. Mama had invited her doctor friend to our
apartment.

"I'm Canadian, like bacon," he said, and we all laughed and made
noises like pigs. He was tall and thin and pale. His hands were soft and
damp when they touched my face looking for traces of my mother. He
moved like a ghost around our tiny rooms. I lay down on the bed with
the door open and pretended to be asleep. He and Mama sat at the
kitchen table drinking from a big bottle of whiskey. Mama started
dancing around the apartment followed by the doctor. The doctor
asked her to take off her uniform. She unbuttoned three top buttons

before dancing into the bedroom and falling onto the bed with me. He took out a camera and started taking pictures of us, but mostly of Mama in her pink satin slip. She laughed a lot that night, but she cried some too after the doctor left. I wonder if she is with the doctor now.

In the suitcase there are three letters from my father, Matisse Santos. They are addressed to my mother in Kansas. The light blue envelopes are identical with dark blue and red edges and pretty stamps from Mexico. They are tied with a shiny black ribbon. Inside the first envelope is a small painting on a flat square of wood wrapped in tissue paper, of a naked woman the color of a tangerine. The woman looks like my mother. At that moment I begin to suffer my mother's absence and ache for my father. A poem is written on the back of the painting in a steady hand, in two languages:

*The poet Guillén once wrote:*

*Un río de promesas*
*baja de tus cabellos . . .*

*A river of promises*
*falls from your hair . . .*

My father's voice haunts me, does violence to my heart. The second letter is written to me:

*October 1*

*Angelita Mariah,*
*Your papa is in Mexico painting pictures and houses near the ocean. Your mother has promised to bring you here so that we can begin to know each other. She says you are in school, that you can read. I wish I could have taught you.*

*Maybe I can teach you other things. I am sending you a picture so that you will know me. I also send you my love. We'll be together someday.*

*Your father, Matisse Santos*

It is as if my father is speaking to me, as if no time has passed and he has sprung up whole from the earth with the long-awaited promise of togetherness. A small photo falls from the folds in the letter onto my lap. The photo is of a shirtless man, wearing beach shorts, standing in front of the ocean. He is smiling. He is beautiful. I look for any trace of blue paint on his body, any trace of me. The last envelope is filled with ashes. I am startled by the pool of tears that well up in my eyes and spill down the front of my dress. I feel as if I have lost a whole life and am preparing for a new one. Before this moment I was never sure if my father was human or simply a complicated design of my mother's imagination. I have in my hands proof of his existence and his love for me. I want to be with him more than anything.

Playing Rosemary soothes me while I wait for my aunts in the living room. The cello and I, we make the sound of trees falling, wind blowing, bare feet on broken glass. We sweep the air with our mourning.

When my aunts come home I am still wearing my pajamas. The green suitcase of evidence lies open next to me. Aunt Faith has one foot on the stair and is calling my name when she takes in the sight of me. We size each other up like boxers before a match. Aunt Merleen almost bumps into her from behind. We stare at each other to see who will blink first. "A bit dog will holler," Aunt Merleen has always said and she is true to her word when she speaks first, attempting to defend herself with weak excuses for keeping my life from me.

"You had no business going through our things . . ."

"Does my father still write me letters?" I clutch the blue envelopes to my chest.

"That was years ago. He hasn't written you since you been with us."
Aunt Merleen avoids my eyes.

"He called here once or twice," Aunt Faith admits.

"Why didn't you tell me?" I ask slowly, evenly, though I am trembling inside.

"Wasn't nothing to tell. He just wanted to know if you were all right. You're all right here with us." Aunt Faith fusses with the belt at her waist.

"We thought she was coming back." Aunt Merleen shadowboxes with me.

"It wasn't our place." Aunt Faith's voice is weak, almost scared.

My eyes cut a path to the front door. I imagine myself running past them into the street and somewhere out there finding the road that leads to my real life with this new father I've found who has pledged his love for me. Instead I continue to sit on the sofa with Rosemary between my legs. I wrap my arms around her body and press my face against her cool, smooth surface. I close my eyes and listen in case I need to go someplace else, in case what they tell me is too hard to bear. Finally, reluctantly, voices overlapping, Aunt Faith and Aunt Merleen sing.

"Your mother . . ." Faith begins, her lips trembling. "This pains me to tell you this."

"Is a drug addict," Merleen says.

"Was in trouble . . ." Faith tries to finish the story. "When she come to us she was all tore up over some married doctor. She was pregnant by him. When he said he was leaving her, your mother got hysterical. The doctor started giving her drugs to calm her down. When he left her for good, she started taking drugs from the hospital. They threatened to take you away from her. She begged them to let her bring you to us."

My insides shiver. I can tell by her hesitations that between each new declaration are still more secrets she tries desperately to hide. She has become a faded length of lace I can see straight through.

"She didn't *want* to be found. Baby, to tell you the truth she called here a couple of times and didn't seem to be herself. We told her you're doing fine. We told her how well you doing in school and how pretty you play the cello."

"Where is she now?" I ask, afraid of hearing the dark clouds in their throat.

"Last we heard she was in a clinic trying to pull herself together. She left before she was supposed to. She sent for you but her counselor said she wasn't ready yet. She left there and we haven't spoken to her in a while. She didn't want you to know all this." Aunt Faith sighs and slips off her Sunday shoes arranging them neatly beside her chair.

"What about her diary?" My grip tightens on Rosemary's neck, the strings bite into my skin.

My aunts exchange looks. Merleen answers, "It was never meant for you to see."

"It would only have disgraced your mother if anything happened to her." Faith looks away as if remembering all the shameful words she'd swallowed with her eyes.

"She's not dead. Just because you haven't heard from her, it doesn't mean she's dead. You didn't have no right to destroy what she wrote."

I can hear the kitchen clock ticking too loudly. Every little sound, each spot of color and new word falling from their lips seems to scratch at my skin.

"Little Coral was a good baby, never give nobody a minute's worth of trouble." Aunt Faith is sitting in her chair still wearing her Sunday hat. She seems to be talking to the vase of yellow gladiolas on top of the piano.

Merleen's heavy stocking feet are pacing a pattern into the carpet. Faith is near tears, but she won't look at me. Neither of them will look at me. I feel like shaking all the fruit from their tree. I want them to hurt like me. Aunt Merleen re-crosses her steps well out of my reach. Her voice is too loud in its attempt to shift my attention from their silent lies and evil deeds. "She didn't want you to see all of that."

"What about my father?" My voice cracks, tears form behind my eyes shut tight.

My father, they tell me, is an unstable painter who lives in Los Angeles.

"Why didn't he come for me?" I scream, suddenly losing my grip on Rosemary. The cello crashes to the carpet with a loud thump.

"We didn't know nothing about him. We weren't about to send you off to some man we never met without your mother's permission. He's a bachelor. And your mother, when she asked for you a few months back, she wasn't ready, her counselor said she wasn't ready," Faith repeats.

I am a storm spiraling through the room breaking bowls and glasses.

I open every drawer in the china cabinet and turn the contents onto the carpet.

"Where is she? Where is she?" I scream curses, tear the Sunday paper to shreds, scratch the paint off the wall and moan and cry. Aunt Merleen grabs my arms and holds me away from her. She is as strong as she looks.

"We asked your mama if we could have you," Aunt Faith says. She has moved to the doorway, her hat in her hand.

"Have me?" My body freezes in Merleen's hands.

"Adopt you. But she wouldn't sign the papers. She say she's coming back when she gets herself together."

I am stunned. The truth is like a hammer to my heart. I don't belong to anybody. I am an undelivered package, an extra piece of toast, something no one wants but can't be thrown away.

"We got this last week." Faith hands me a letter she pulls from her Sunday pocketbook.

It is a note from my mother. In her shaky handwriting she has written: *Give this to my baby and tell her that I love her.* A small square of pale pink paper floats onto my lap. It is blank, but I can see the imprint of her lips. Cool, invisible fingers caress the back of my neck. I wrap my arms around my body and lean against the wall shivering.

"She's still traveling, baby," Aunt Faith says, resting her hand on my face. I stop resisting, my body goes limp.

"Can't I travel too?" I ask, crumbling in her arms.

"We want you here with us," Faith whispers into my hair.

It is not enough, I think. It is not a mother's love or a father's love. I hate my mother for leaving me so alone in the world.

"I want to talk to my father," I say, the idea growing large in my mind as his blue spattered image comes alive.

In the kitchen Aunt Faith dials the number. My eyes follow her fingers. I memorize the numbers, raise red welts as I scratch them onto the inside of my arm with the tip of my fingernail. I am anxious and afraid for the sound of my father's voice.

"This is Coral's Aunt Faith. Mariah wants to talk to you." She hands me the phone. It is hot in my hands.

"Daddy?" I whisper, turning away from my aunts' sharp eyes and open ears.

"Mariah. How are you, sweetheart?" His voice is a blues song that turns out all right. He says all the right things. I can feel his fatherly love through the telephone wires all the way from California, and it saves me. I can hardly hear what he is saying because my crying is long and loud. By the end of our first conversation my father has promised to write to me and says he wants to see for himself how I've grown. I cling to his every word as if I am drowning and he is saving me. Later that night I mix the ashes from my father's letter with honey and lick the spoon clean. I imagine that in the letter he asked for me and pledged his love always. I don't leave my room the entire weekend. I play Rosemary silently, not giving my aunts the pleasure of her voice. I find a funeral march in her strings. Memories of life with Mama threaten to undo us both. I can hear my aunts in the hallway whispering angrily. They stand outside the bedroom door listening to me suffer. By morning I am asleep with Rosemary in my arms.

One week later a brown box appears on my bed. It is from my father. Inside the box is a brand-new red, hardcover dictionary, a sketch pad, and a box of sharpened colored pencils. I open the dictionary to the first page and a ten-dollar bill is spread out on the inside cover. Underneath it is an elaborately drawn inscription penned in red ink: *For my daughter Mariah, all my love, your father Matisse.* Below the inscription, a drawing of a man reading a book to a little girl held on his lap, leaned into the crook of his arm. He is my father, and I am his little girl. Every night I read from the dictionary and find new words that are beautiful to look at, lovely when I sound them out on my tongue. I underline words in red ink. *Promise . . . aspiration . . . fidelity . . . bond . . . palpable . . .* When I find a new word that I think he'll like I draw a picture of it and color it and send it to my father with a few words of my own. We talk on the phone for a few minutes each month and on my birthday and at Christmas he sends me a big brown box. Inside is a dress that is always too small or too large. Aunt Faith alters them and I only wear them to church on Sunday. He sends me colored paper and pens and picture books with no words. Each month he sends my aunts an envelope with money in it. Sometimes I feel like a prisoner. I want to escape to where paradise must be, with my father.

*L*ater that summer a bright red flower of blood stains my underwear. Aunt Faith had warned me that this day would come and shown me the drawer in the bathroom where I will find supplies each month. She seems ashamed and won't look me in the eye as she gives me brief instructions on how to care for my new body and keep myself clean. But I am the one who feels shame, as if I have done something dirty.

"This means you're a woman now. Take care how you act around men. You could get in trouble," she says, pausing after each commandment to make sure I appreciate the weight of her words. I stare at the bottle of white vinegar standing between us on the kitchen table. I wonder if she means my father too.

"When I was a young girl folks didn't really talk about this. We tore up sheets to use for your time of the month. Now they got books to explain things. If you got any questions you can just look it up in here." She puts a thin pamphlet on the table and leaves me sitting there staring at it.

Joy's sister Nicky has already told me what this event really means. She says that if I kiss a boy I like, I can have a baby. My mother should be here to tell me these things. I have started writing words on the wall behind the bed. I lie on my stomach on the cool wooden floor, under the rusty metal springs, with a pencil in my hand. I write in tiny print, letters to my mother and my father, my last will and testament, a song, my favorite colors and the names of my two best friends, Rosemary and Joy, neither of whom can hold me now. I write in the dark to see what will come of it in the light.

I wear dresses so that underneath I can live in my mother's pink satin skin. I press my hands over my small breasts and down the length of my body over and over again until I can feel my mother's breasts rising beneath the cool pink satin. I want to believe she put me here for safekeeping, that I am her treasure. I am comforted for now by these little things.

*Every night I take my mother's hand and we walk down the front stairs as if she'd never left me. We walk out the front door and along the railroad tracks, catching lightning bugs in the cup of our hands and letting them go. On these night visits, we do not speak, yet we understand each other completely.*

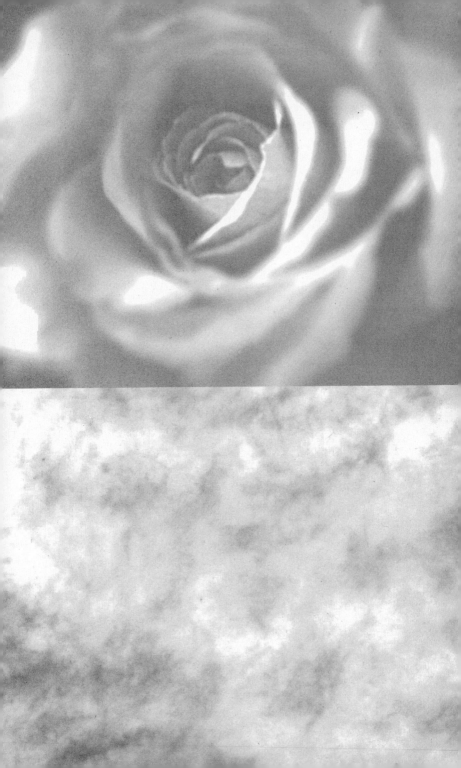

SIX

*I*t becomes easier to hang out with Joy when we start seventh grade at the junior high school beyond the cemetery, across the railroad tracks, down past the cracker factory. Even though we are forbidden to see each other, me and the girly-girl meet at the railroad crossing and walk to school together every morning. Our first day of school is special this year because we are going to O. Williams Junior High School with eighth and ninth graders, and for the first time we will be going to school with white kids, by law. On the base in Manhattan, Kansas, I remember going to school with all kinds of kids and nobody made a big deal out of it, but things are different here in the south. Aunt Merleen and Aunt Faith have warned me about minding my manners. The minister even preached a sermon about race relations and how we are all colors, all kinds, God's children in his eyes. Old, out of breath white men with thick southern accents scream red-faced at reporters and anybody watching the evening news to beware the return of northern agitators and nigger-loving radicals, whoever they are. White mothers and fathers clutch wide-eyed children to them like their last possessions and swear that they will fight this plan to convert their children to Communism. I thought communism was a new religion. Aunt Merleen and Aunt Faith told me not to pay attention to all the fuss.

"Your only concern is to study hard and make something out of yourself," Aunt Faith said, passing me a needle to thread for her.

"All the rest don't mean squat." Aunt Merleen turned the tv off and started reading the newspaper.

The red brick school I attended since I was seven years old was all black, from freckle-faced, banana-colored Dwight James in my class to indigo blue-black Mr. Champion, the principal. The vice principal and the secretary and the teachers, all the ladies who worked in the lunchroom, the custodian, and all of us kids were black. In addition to reading, writing, and arithmetic we have been taught not to embarrass the race by our behavior, to succeed not only for our parents and ourselves but for the entire Negro race. Parents were called at home if we did not act like the little ladies and gentlemen we were supposed to become. Often the teachers were told to whip the palms of our hands with straps and short wooden rulers if we acted up. In rare cases the parents were called into school to beat their child in front of the class as an example to the rest of us to obey without question. Our teachers had high expectations of us. You are the future, they repeated over and over again. One of those teachers was Mrs. Towns, a tall, slim older woman who wore a short brown wig that stuck out at the back of her neck and such a thick dusting of powder on her face we called her "Dough Face" behind her back. Mrs. Towns stayed after school with me every afternoon for weeks until I learned fractions. She said it was her job to make sure I had the basic tools to succeed in life. "It's hard enough being a Negro. You must be better than good. You must excel, Mariah," she said as if she were making a speech. At first it felt like I was being punished, but when I caught on to how fractions worked I almost hugged that powdered old woman. She just smiled and told me not to get a big head.

So Joy and I, we do not know what to expect on our first day of being integrated. We have seen Governor George Wallace repeatedly on tv standing in the schoolhouse door over in Alabama to keep black kids from sitting next to white kids. We wonder if we will be on the news. We hold hands like we used to, as we walk along the tracks, singing like Aretha on her new forty-five. Not many white kids show up on the first day. The three buses are only half-filled with long-faced boys and girls dressed like us in new school clothes and attitude. O. Williams is still mostly made up of black kids who live in the projects or in apartments and houses two miles down the road from the school, next to the slaughterhouse. Joy and I are in different homerooms, but we promise to meet at the end of the day in the bathroom near the far end of the school.

Almost everything is the same. The Lord's Prayer. The Pledge of Allegiance to the flag. Roll call. Our teacher, though, is a young white woman with long straight blonde hair and turtle green eyes. The top of her head barely reaches the middle of the blackboard. She looks as young as Joy's sister Nicky, who is not even sixteen yet, and she looks scared too.

"Good morning, class. My name is Miss Phillips. Today is a special day and I'd like to get us started on the right foot by helping us get to know each other." She even sounds like a little girl. Her voice is high and thin and shakes like the last leaf on a winter bush. When she tells us to push our chairs against the wall, forming a circle around the room, we do it. We stand by our desks and watch her get down on her knees and use white chalk to draw a ragged outline of a large map of the United States onto the concrete floor while calling out the gulf states on the bottom edge of the map. I have never seen a teacher on her knees. She stands up, dusts off her navy blue skirt, and goes back to her desk.

"I want you all to stand on the place on the map where you were born."

We all shuffle to the place we think is Georgia. Everyone has an opinion, but finally we all agree on where we think it is. A thin white girl wearing a red sweater with holes in one sleeve stands alone in Florida.

"Good," Miss Phillips says, smiling. "Now introduce yourself to somebody you don't know and tell them where you'd like to live someday."

Nobody wants to be the first so I go down to Florida and tell the little white girl in one quick breath that I want to live in Mexico so I can swim in the ocean every day. At first she doesn't say anything. Then looking around as if she is being watched, she whispers, "My name's Maryann. I'm not supposed to talk to colored people, but I want to live in North Carolina with my grandma because she lives on a farm with real chickens."

Right then everybody starts talking and the teacher has to stand on a chair to get us to quiet down.

"Now, class, imagine that this map is now a map of the city. This is the river east, downtown west, the mall north, and the highway south. Go stand in the place where you live now."

And we separate, Maryann and I, as we do each afternoon when school is out, into black and white. I watch her from across the room and wonder if I'll ever know more than her name.

"Let's talk about what integration means," Miss Phillips begins.

All is not calm in our new universe. A fight breaks out on the first day of school. I find out from Joy in the lunchroom over dry beans, sticky rice, and brown meat smothered in gravy.

"Jew Baby got sent to the office before the first bell rang," Joy says, then swallows from a carton of chocolate milk with her head thrown back.

"His name is Samson," I say, trying to find the meat under the gravy.

"Whatever. His sister is gonna be mad if she have to come all the way over here to get him." Joy's fork is moving so fast food flies onto the table. She probably didn't get anything more to eat than the red cherry rocket pop I gave her this morning on the way to school.

"What happened?" I ask, pushing my tray toward her. I watch her clean my plate. She talks with her mouth full, so I have to ask her to repeat some things.

She tells me that as a joke Samson picked up a white girl waiting out in the hall for classes to start and raised her over his head. He's done that to me a few times since he's grown almost a head taller and a foot wider than me over the past two summers. I would yell at him and beat him on his big square head until he put me down, but this girl he raised above his head like a muscleman's Q-tip has a brother who threw Samson against a wall. Samson's friends jumped into it and all hell broke loose. Samson was always getting into trouble trying to live up to his name.

The next thing that happened is that Joy found a ring on the second-floor bathroom sink. She shows it to me under the table.

"Are you gonna take it to the office?" I ask her, staring at the pretty red birthstone ring in the palm of her hand.

"You crazy. If it was so important whoever lost it wouldn't have. I'll take good care of it," Joy says, putting it in the pocket of her tight flowered dress. "I never had anything this pretty in my life." I don't say anything. My aunts taught me never to take anything that didn't belong to me, but I can see Joy's point. To Joy, the ring is left for her as a gift by a careless hand.

As if that were not enough, before the three o'clock bell rings for our release, Joy puts gum in a white girl's hair. The white girl sits in front of her and keeps tossing her long dark curls over her shoulder onto Joy's desk, time after time brushing the top of Joy's paper. Joy pushes several pieces of bubble gum into her mouth and finally blows a big bubble and lets it pop in the girl's hair, then mashes the rest of the huge wad into the girl's scalp as she screams murder. When Joy gets suspended for a week I'm mad because I don't have anybody to hang out with.

Neicey goes to school here too, but she is still stuck up. She hangs out with the white kids and barely speaks to me when she sees me in the hall. I wish I could talk to Mr. Giovanni about white people, but I know what he would say: "We are all equal in the sight of God." But we *are* different. We like different music, we live in different places, eat different foods, and go to different churches.

One day when Miss Phillips is out sick, a substitute teacher named Mrs. Peabody arrives. Like Miss Phillips she is young and white. But her hair is brown and thin and hangs lifeless around her long face. Because she never smiles, her face does not seem pretty. Her wool suit is tight around her neck and she has a run in her thick brown stockings. She asks Maryann what is the lesson for the day. When Maryann doesn't answer she asks a boy from the projects who doesn't answer. When she asks me her eyes have become daggers of flame. I ignore her and continue to write words that aren't words, but letters joined in thought on the wooden surface of my desk in blue ink. *Siaijd* . . . *ownciuy* . . . *tyoijow* . . . *nvgvvd* . . . *qoriuf* . . .

"Are you stupid?" she asks, as if I will answer her. I ignore her like everyone else, but I am the one she decides to punish by sending to the Special Education class. Special Ed is where they put the retarded kids with the kids who have trouble spelling, with the kids who scream all day, with the kids in wheelchairs, with the kids who can't read, with the kids who talk too much, with the kids who pee in their pants, with the kids who like to pick fights, with the kids who pick their noses, with the kids like me whose spirit needs to be broken. When I walk into the Special Ed classroom in the basement of the building the teacher, a black man with a mustache, is holding a girl's arm away from her as if the girl would hit herself with the ruler in her hand if he let her. There are no white kids in Special Ed. Everyone else in the classroom is either making noise or talking to somebody else. I see another regular kid on punishment. It is Tree. Deadman's half sister Tree is a project girl. Everybody calls her Tree but her name is Teresa. Deadman, Joy told me, had been arrested by the time he was fourteen for breaking a policeman's nose. He'd come home from juvenile detention with knife scars on his neck. Deadman got his name because of his grandfather. He used to sleep with his grandfather. When he was five years old he woke up in the middle of the night from a nightmare. His grandfather had died, but Deadman thought he was sleeping so he crawled closer to the old man and went back to sleep. His grandfather was known to rise with the chickens, so the next morning, when he didn't come down for breakfast, they found Deadman asleep in his grandfather's arms. They called him Deadman from that day to this and everybody who knows him will swear that he can speak to dead people in his dreams. People beg him not to dream about them because if he does you are almost always in the hands of spirits within a day or two. Deadman saw his father being killed in his dreams and within a few months his father was killed by a train at the railyard where he worked. Tree is the quiet one. I often see her passing my house and jealously watch as she walks along holding her mother's hand.

Tree is reading a magazine at a desk in the back of the class. She looks up and calls me over to her. Her voice is low and heavy like cigarette smoke.

"What are you in for?" she asks, folding the magazine up and sticking it in her back pocket.

"Armed robbery. You?"

"Murder in the first degree," she says, and we laugh.

I find out that she has been here for a week. She is in because her teacher said she was talking to herself. Tree said she was reciting a poem she made up so she wouldn't forget it. The teacher didn't believe her.

"You're Deadman's sister?" I ask.

"Guilty." She raises her right hand in the air.

"How did you get a name like Tree?" I ask boldly.

"My brother's got a lazy tongue. When we was little he couldn't say Teresa. Said he wanted a baby brother anyway. He says I'm a pretty good brother for a girl. I can kick his ass playing basketball." She laughs, dribbles an invisible basketball, then tosses it gracefully into the air.

"You don't live in the projects, do you?" she asks.

"No. I live in the big white house across the tracks."

"Don't be confused, just because you live across the street from us. You still a project girl."

The days I spend in Special Ed with Tree I learn some things I'll never forget. Tree's mama is a union organizer and she teaches Tree and Deadman things they don't teach you in school. Tree says that's why her brother is always in trouble fighting all the time. He's mad because their mama has taught them that life isn't fair for black people. According to Tree, according to her mama, in our world, the house you live in, the clothes you wear, the books you read don't make you special with white people if you're black or with rich people if you're poor.

Tree and I don't hang out after this week—she is an upperclass-man—but she is a kind face I can count on for a wink or smile when she sees me in the hall or the lunchroom, even when she is with her friends. Most times when I see her, she is alone and almost always her lips are moving as if she is trying to remember another poem. Her acknowledgment makes me feel special, like I belong somewhere.

Joy and I, we don't pay attention much in class and barely pass any of them except P.E. We are always late for school because we sneak into the girls' bathroom before school to talk and giggle and make plans together. We make each other up with pale green eye shadow, dark blue eyeliner, and hot pink lip gloss.

Joy dips her pinky finger into the small pot of sticky frosted glaze and applies it to my lips. It feels as if she is touching me somewhere under my skirt. She makes me press my lips together and spread the slickness over both lips. My hands are shaking when I do her. She looks into my eyes and I know she knows why. She puts her hand on mine to steady me. I try to put my old feelings aside. We are both consid-ered fast by the time we are thirteen, undoing our braids and teasing our loose ponytails into afro puffs that stick out from our heads like nappy sponges. Joy talks about boys a lot. She thinks Deadman is cute. I think his half sister Tree is cuter, but I don't tell Joy this. We talk a lot about running away together, but I worry that when my mama comes back she won't know where to find me. In the afternoons me and the girly-girl linger in front of the bathroom mirror wiping down our faces with Vaseline and combing our hair back into neat orderly braids.

I want so bad to tell Joy about my mother and show her the pic-ture of my father. I want to tell her everything, but it's hard to talk about my mama because even the word *mother* makes my throat close up and tears come to my eyes. It's almost as if she were dead. I want to tell her about the letters from my father but I let the girly-girl talk instead. Let her tell me her secrets. She knows that I will never tell.

When Joy tells me that she is pregnant, I nearly choke on my fork full of Jell-O salad. In six months, she says, she will have someone to love her completely. I want this too. She tells me that she is in love with a man named Willie T. Lovell. He is a grown man, nineteen years old and driving his own car. She shows me pictures of him and he does looks fine in his soldier uniform. He is from Virginia, but he is stationed at the army base just up the highway.

"We met downtown at the skating rink on Nigger Night. He thought I was eighteen," she says, lighting up a cigarette by the window after lunch in the bathroom.

"Don't use that word." I take the cigarette from her hand and inhale.

"Everybody calls it that. You're too religious." She crosses her legs and starts rubbing on her belly like she can feel the baby moving around in there.

"What's religion got to do with it?"

"Anyway, like I was saying. He let me talk to his mama on the telephone. Now that's serious."

I am only a little jealous, but I pretend to be happy for her.

"He's gonna marry me when the baby comes. We're going overseas and I'm gonna have my own apartment. Mrs. Joyous Lovell." She does a little dance twirling like a ballerina.

"You gonna finish school?"

"What for? My man got a job with the government. Girl, you better get yourself a man if you ever want to get out of this town. Willie's got a cousin who'll take you out."

"That's all right." I am embarassed that she thinks she has to find somebody for me.

"If you don't hurry up and get a boyfriend people gonna think you funny or something." It seems her memory of our kisses are gone as completely as mine are safe. She takes the last drag off the cigarette and flips it into the toilet by the door several feet away.

"I'm gonna have me a baby. If that nig . . . if Willie T. ever leave me I'll always have something of my own," she says, already thousands of miles away from me.

The idea, once planted, grows inside me like a seed. I start looking for a man to make me a river of promises, to stain me with passion. I want an angel in my arms.

SEVEN

It is summer, I am fourteen years old. I have waited but my father has not come for me. He no longer offers excuses and I don't expect them. I have outgrown the adventures between the pages of the picture books he sends me. Instead of going to church on Sundays, I go to Governors Park by myself to watch baseball games. Aunt Merleen always says, "God gives you two eyes, one to keep on what you have, and one to keep on what you want." The whole month of July I keep both eyes on the back gate at Golden Park looking for number twenty-two, my lucky number according to the psychic who sits in the window under the sign of the blue hand on Fourth Street. I don't know what I am thinking. Maybe I hope that he will notice me out of all the other girls waiting around after the baseball game, looking for a number. Dark hair, dark eyes settled in a kind, brown face. Lips that speak Spanish. I imagine that he will teach me things, give me things, take me away from it all. Four o'clock, Saturday, July thirteenth, Jesus Miguel Monteverde, number twenty-two, outfielder for the Astros' farm team, looks me dead in the eye and smiles. He throws a baseball to me, underhand. I catch it and throw it back in a high arc that makes us both stretch our necks. In midair the baseball turns into a perfect orange which he gives to me along with a single word, *naranja*.

I've watched girls catch baseballs from other players for four weeks and I know that he is choosing me. I was told never to speak to strangers, but when Jesus Miguel takes me by the hand, I follow him to the steak house across the street. He eats hunched over his food like a starving animal. Wolfing down a huge steak and french fries like he hasn't eaten in days. I sip sour chianti and nibble at the cold french fries at the edge of his plate like I'm not hungry. I'm not sure he'll buy me dinner so I drink the water the waitress plops down in front of each of us and refill the glass with chianti every chance I get, trying to look eighteen and wondering what Joy would do.

I find out from the baseball program the ladies' room attendant has let me read that he is from the Dominican Republic. I don't speak Spanish and he only speaks a few words of English so we spend a lot of time looking into each other's eyes, smiling shyly. Somehow we understand each other. His hand is dancing a merengue with my left hand on the red vinyl space between us in the booth. I can't breathe and my breasts seem to grow when he touches me.

It is a short walk to the hotel downtown where Jesus Miguel lives during baseball season. The evening air is warm and sticky as we walk hand in hand along the deserted streets. I try to put the thought of Aunt Faith and Aunt Merleen waiting for me out of my mind. I don't want to go back, not the same me that left the big white house right after breakfast with nothing but a crisp new ten-dollar bill from my father in my pocket. I want something to happen, some great change to fit the new me that woke up with a new body, new ways of seeing things, and new feelings I don't yet have a name for. Jesus Miguel kisses me sweetly on the cheek and waves good-bye as he walks through the doors into his hotel.

"It's nine o'clock at night! Where have you been?" Aunt Merleen's anger greets me at the back door. Aunt Faith is standing right behind her. I squeeze past them and open the refrigerator to pour myself a glass of water.

"We were worried. We thought something happened to you," Aunt Faith says to my back.

"I'm okay. I took the long way home." I drink the cool water in quick sips.

"You are not grown. It is too late for you to be coming in this house," she says.

"I'm sorry," I say as I rinse my glass in the sink. I try to walk past them up the back stairs. Aunt Merleen is shaking when she lays her hand on my shoulder. She growls near my face.

"I want you in this house before dark every night. Do you understand?" Aunt Faith watches us from her seat at the kitchen table. Her eyes are sad.

"I understand," I say, but I have been marked. I understand how a kiss can make a rose bloom. Jesus Miguel Monteverde has made me want to run out into the humid night and get lost in the center of a soul kiss.

I dream about Jesus Miguel every day of the week. The following Sunday afternoon when my aunts leave for the nursing home I walk down to the baseball park. It is a long boring game. Jesus Miguel strikes out both times at bat and the game ends tied 1–1. After the game I go downstairs to wait. The players haven't come out yet but several girls are waiting, clinging to the chain-link fence with painted nails the color of summer melons. I watch for number twenty-two and I am not disappointed. Jesus Miguel walks out of the dressing room wearing a white tee shirt and neatly pressed jeans. He is tall and broad-shouldered, someone I can lean on without fear of falling. This time he buys me dinner at the restaurant across the street. He plays with my hand under the table. We walk to his hotel and, with him still holding my hand, we walk inside together. The desk clerk follows us with his eyes, but he doesn't say anything. In the elevator I can hear my heart beating. I wonder if Jesus Miguel can hear it too. We walk side by side down the carpeted hall without speaking. He turns the key in the lock and I am lost.

Inside his room there are two twin beds neatly made up with light blue bedspreads. The dresser is cluttered with loose change, sports magazines, an orange, and two-for-one coupons from local restaurants. There is a glass of water and a phone on the bedside table, and a laminated card with the Virgin Mary on it. My head starts spinning so I sit down on one of the beds. Jesus Miguel takes a shower while I flip through the channels on the color tv. I am strangely calm. I eat the orange, a deep burgundy color inside. The juice drips down my arm and onto the bed staining it like blood, *sangre.* I even eat the peel which tastes like flowers, *flores.* He comes out of the bathroom wearing boxer shorts. He stands there in the doorway looking at me for a long time. He shows me a picture of his sister. "Rosa. *Mi hermana,*" he says softly.

Looking at her picture is like looking in a mirror. My eyes, my hair, the shape of my lips. He makes me understand that he misses her. I understand that we both have a need to be filled this evening. I turn off the tv, and we lie down together on one of the tiny beds in the dark, look out of the window, and count the stars. *Estrella de Noche,* he calls me, Night Star. He puts his arms around me and starts singing the sweetest song I've ever heard. I don't understand the words, they are all in Spanish, but the meaning is clear, *claro.* I close my eyes and he kisses me, softly, sweetly on my left cheek. In his arms I feel safe, wanted, wise to have chosen him. I kiss him on the lips and feel a slow shock of lightening snake through our bodies. I clench my thighs to hold this feeling. Our clothes peel away like the skin of the orange. With my tongue I paint his neck and hairless chest, take him in my mouth until he pushes me away gently. His hands leave a trail of fingerprints on my body in all directions. His damp kisses down my thighs make my body reach for him. He separates my legs with his large, smooth hands, then eases a finger inside me, dipping it back and forth. It feels good, and I'm not scared anymore. When he finally enters me, I bite into the thick muscle of his shoulder and cry a little. He rocks and stirs in me until he can no longer hold back. I hold him inside me long after he comes, hoping that this small pain will turn into a perfect little girl who will love me. We fall asleep and dream the same dreams.

*We live in a pale blue house with a red tiled roof next to an orchard of blooming lemon trees. Our children are stars that glow in a navy blue sky. Jesus Miguel rubs my feet with mint leaves. With my tongue I tattoo his back with a bouquet of red and orange flowers. Our children sing like angels above the trees. They sing to us in Spanish. Only dreams,* Solo sueños.

My eyes can still find his features in the dark. He seems to me everything beautiful and magic and good. I listen for the music of his voice in my dreams. *Que sueñes con los angelitos.* We are both dreaming with the angels.

*E*very night locked in my room, alone in my bed, I feel my stomach, searching for our baby. I squeeze my nipples checking for milk, stick my finger, dipped in honey, inside myself to feed the baby if it is there. If there is life in my belly, it will be a girl, I am sure. A little girl who is more beautiful than a star. I will name her Estrella. Estrella de Noche. I will feed her honey from a silver spoon and I will love her and she will learn to love me, because it is what I need.

I keep trying to sneak out to see Jesus Miguel, to be with him, but my aunts lock me in my room at night. When I wasn't home by midnight they called the police, who called the ballpark, who called the hotel clerk, who called Jesus Miguel's room to warn us that the police were on their way. In the shower I held him tight and didn't let go for a long time. He stroked my hair and said sweet things to me in Spanish. He dried my body, then kissed each part tenderly. He dressed me, then gave me money for a taxi home. When we parted in front of the hotel there was no need for promises. I had a mouth full of Spanish kisses and when I closed my eyes I saw dark-eyed laughing babies who looked like Jesus playing among the stars.

My aunts threatened to have Jesus Miguel arrested for kidnapping. They throw up their hands, call on God, and finally they ignore me, and this suits me fine. The only words I have are for my baby-to-be. Rosemary and I make up songs.

I don't want to get him in trouble, but I am so lonely. I just want to see him one more time. One night when the house is asleep, I steal slowly down the back stairs, careful to avoid the noisy step near the bottom. I feel around in the dark for the keys to the big blue car. My heart is beating so loudly it seems to be shaking the floor beneath my feet. Just as my hand reaches for the cold bits of metal, the fluorescent kitchen light snaps on. I snatch my hand away and try not to look guilty of the crime I was about to commit.

"I see you can't sleep either." Aunt Merleen is in her long johns and night cap. She looks tired.

"I was just going out to sit on the porch." The lie falls easily out of my mouth.

"Sit down here with me for a minute," she says patiently, pulling up a chair to the kitchen table. She sounds out of breath.

I reluctantly sit across from her, playing with the rooster-shaped salt shaker. A little salt spills on the slick white tablecloth. I throw a pinch over my shoulder. Merleen laughs.

"Your mama used to do that," she says, smiling briefly.

I don't say a word.

"Where were you going tonight? To see that ball player? Baby, he don't mean you no good. He's gonna get you in trouble with a big stomach like that girlfriend of yours."

I refuse to look at her.

"You are not to go over there to Governors Park," she says. It is almost a plea. How can she forbid me to see the man who has changed me forever, the one who will give me something of my own to love?

"Don't break my heart. You're so much like your mama. Don't start traveling too soon or you'll never be at rest. Your mama was catching trains and running away from home when she was your age and it didn't lead to no good. We couldn't do nothing about her life with Gert but we can do something for you. Don't you break my heart, child," she says, as if it is broken already. I don't want to hurt my aunts. I wish I could make them understand that I need someone of my own. Like Aunt Merleen has Aunt Faith, like my mother had my father, I want someone just for me.

There is a blue thread in the hem of the dish towel drying over the sink. I try to drown out her voice with the heartbeat of my perfect baby girl who will smell like oranges and flowers. I count her toes and fingers in my mind, until Aunt Merleen leaves me sitting at the table in the dark.

My period comes as usual in a gentle flood, two weeks later. For the rest of the summer my aunts watch me closely. I am forced to go with them everywhere, to church, to the nursing home, to the grocery store, to choir rehearsal, and they threaten to send me to Girl Scout camp in Alabama. I follow them, let them watch me because I don't really have anywhere else to go. Jesus Miguel made no promises and I asked for none. At the end of baseball season Jesus Miguel flies back to the Dominican Republic and I know I will probably never see or hear from him again.

"*Y*our mama called this morning after you and Merleen went to the store," Aunt Faith says. "She says she's coming home."

I stop breathing and try to rewind what she has just said. I try to make sense of her words. I put down my fork full of mashed potatoes, go up the stairs, into my room, and pack up everything that means something to me, and that isn't much. I sit on the front stairs every evening to wait for her. The green suitcase sits by my bedroom door for the next three weeks collecting dust. What day did she say she was coming? Where was she calling from? Maybe she was hurt? What could be keeping her from me?

Aunt Faith reaches for my hand across the kitchen table and holds it in hers stroking it gently for a while.

*Beloved . . . possession . . . sweep . . . peace . . . home . . .*

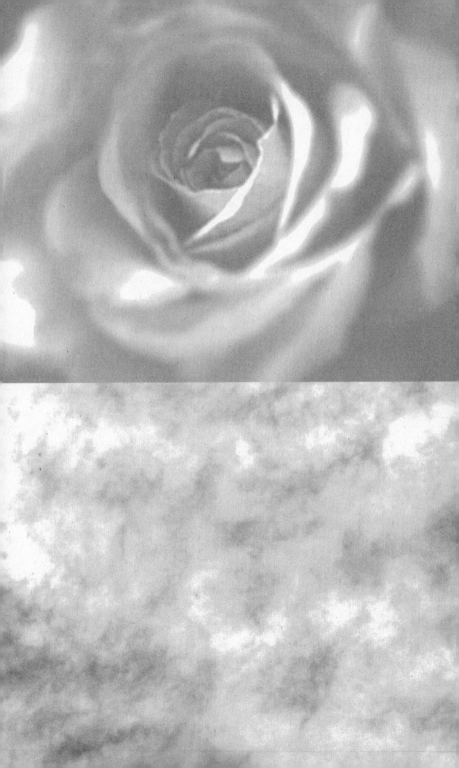

# EIGHT

*I* almost don't recognize Joy running toward me. I am on my way home from school chewing on vocabulary words and phrases from Spanish One.

*Where is my mother? ¿Dónde está mi madre? Who is my father? ¿Quién es mi padre? When? ¿Cuándo . . . ? ¿Cuándo . . . ?*

I haven't seen the girly-girl for weeks. She is fat with the baby. Her big round stomach is half hidden underneath her too-tight blouse. I can almost see the baby straining against her skin, stretched over her belly like leather on a baseball as she runs to me.

"Come on, Myra. They getting ready to march." She chews up my name in her mouth and grabs at me, pulling me toward her.

I give her bare belly a blank look, unable to make sense of what she is trying to tell me between the sight of her and the ragged sound of her gasping for words out of her reach.

"Who's marching? What for?" I ask, my hand on her arm to steady her. She leans forward to catch her breath, then drags me behind her toward the crowd of people running in the direction of downtown. I manage to shake loose from her grip. She turns around to face me and I see that she has been crying.

"Are you okay?" I am scared now, I have never seen her cry.

"You know my cousin Warren?"

I nod yes. He is a tall, lanky boy with a star-shaped gold tooth. He is always working on a broken-down car in her front yard with her stepfather. He always calls me Red and winks at me whenever I walk past her house.

"He's in jail and . . ." She starts crying again. "And Jew Baby's dead. The police shot him in the back. We gonna march this time."

Samson dead. The only other dead person I know is Mr. Giovanni and he was old. I didn't know the two boys the police shot last year who were partying down in the Bottom when Black Maria, the black police van, came through picking up random black men. Everybody said they weren't doing nothing but having a good time. They were just scared to go to jail so they ran. A white policeman shot a fifteen-year-old boy named Peanut in the leg, but Speed wasn't that lucky. They beat him to death when they caught him. Folks got mad and talked about it all summer long, but nothing was done about it. The policeman was never charged. The NAACP planned to march then, but a permit to march was denied. They had a prayer vigil instead that nobody but old folks went to.

By the time we catch up to the growing crowd at the corner of Fourth Street, we can see Reverend Mordell, a short, bald preacher from the Church of Universal Love—Aunt Merleen calls it a storefront operation—trying to calm people down by shouting through a bullhorn.

"The Lord will make a way. Let us pray." Reverend Mordell, chin to chest, bows his head in prayer.

Somebody snatches the bullhorn from him and pushes him aside. It is Deadman. Samson was his best friend.

"White people own everything," he screams through the horn. "They act like they still own us." "Amens" and "right ons" rise up from the crowd. "I ain't no nigger and I don't want to be stomped to death under some white man's boot who's calling me one." There is a charge in the air that is beginning to smell like the start of a fire that will burn out of control.

Deadman gives the bull horn to Danita, Samson's weary-eyed older sister who has children my age. She seems to be even thinner and more hollow than the last time I'd seen her months ago, shelling peas on her front porch.

"We can't let them keep killing our children. Jew Baby was a good boy, y'all know that," she says simply, then puts the horn down on the ground, gently as if it were a child's arm. My throat tightens. I am sad for her, because I know she loved him. She was the one to pay for his piano lessons from Aunt Faith. She came to the back door of the big white house at the end of each week to pay Aunt Faith with twelve quarters knotted in a corner of a white handkerchief.

Suddenly she lets go of a loud mournful howl from deep in her belly. The next sound we hear is breaking glass. We turn around and see the plate-glass window of Masterson's Grocery Store gape open like a mouth with ragged glass teeth.

"White people own everything! They act like they still own us! First-rate prices for second-rate produce!" Deadman shouts through the bullhorn. This declaration throws gasoline on the crowd. In a burst of motion Joy and me are pulled into the flow of bodies sucked into the store through the broken window. We grab grocery bags and fill them with Mr. Masterson's second-rate produce, dented canned goods, and questionable meats.

I grab a jar of dill pickles and a handful of Pez candies. I see Deadman's half sister Tree near the cash register. She winks at me as she stuffs her shirt with comic books. It isn't long before we hear sirens. Tree hollers for us to get out. Me and Joy and some others follow her out the back window and drop down into an alley behind the store. Somebody has set the store on fire. We can smell the smoke and see the flames from down the street. We run in a staggered line as if we are in a relay race darting behind thick hedges when searchlights sweep in our path. Tree and Joy leave me in front of the big white house. I watch Joy waddle home with a sack of meat, hugging the edges of the dark buildings, dodging the lights of police cars. Tree cuts down an alley toward the playground with her braids flying behind her.

I try to sneak in through the back door, but Aunt Merleen is sitting at the kitchen table.

"Where have you been?" she demands. "Do you know what's going on out there? We been looking all over for you."

Aunt Faith paces heavily around the kitchen table making the dishes in the china cabinet tremble.

"Samson's dead," I say. "They burned down Masterson's." I shift the heavy sack in my arms.

"That ain't nothing to be proud of. Masterson was high priced, but he didn't kill that boy. He trying to make a living like anybody else."

"Why do you care? You don't shop there," I snap back.

"I can afford not to. Not everybody in this neighborhood has a car to drive all the way over to the A&P." Aunt Faith notices the bag of groceries in my hand.

"There will be no thieves in my house. Give me that." Aunt Merleen snatches the bag from me and throws it in the garbage can underneath the sink.

I run out of the kitchen and up the backstairs to my room. I lie on my bed eating all the Pez candy I'd stuffed in my pockets and I cry for Warren, who might never get out of jail, and I cry for Samson, the prettiest boy I have ever known.

It is calm the day after the march. There is a nine o'clock curfew in the neighborhood. At school all the teachers talk about is the violent behavior of the riot and property damage and all the students talk about is how we fought back. After school I walk by Masterson's store and see that it is burned to the ground. Mr. Masterson is sitting in his car in front of the store looking like he has lost his best friend. I don't go to Samson's funeral because they send his body to Alabama where his mama lives. I write his name on the wall underneath my bed and draw a circle of flames around his name to keep him warm.

There is a change in our neighborhood after Samson dies. The Black Maria police van stops coming to our neighborhood for a while and black people who live in other neighborhoods open little stores and other businesses down the street and sell fresh meats and first-rate produce until an A&P opens a few blocks from where Masterson's has burned down. Joy tells me the NAACP had something to do with getting Samson's sister a job as cashier at the new A&P.

I am only allowed out of the house to go to school and back. Most of the time Aunt Merleen drives me there and picks me up. There is no pleasure in packing my books and hiding makeup in my pencil bag with Joy gone. My body is present in classes but not the rest of me. My mind takes trains and invents words that follow an intimate geography. My distraction shows in my failing grades.

The new teachers at O. Williams, even the black ones, don't seem to care whether or not I master algebra. Aunt Merleen and Aunt Faith care; they arrange countless conferences with my teachers and the vice principal. The principal doesn't bother to see them when they come to the school, he is always too busy coaching the football team to victory. He does send them a letter saying he will expel me from O. Williams if my attitude does not improve. It does not but I keep to myself just how sad and angry I am at the whole world and the universe.

When I run into the girly-girl at the drugstore downtown two months after the march I am afraid of what will happen if I stay in this town. She tells me that her mother put her out after she had her baby, a cute little boy she named Willie T. Lovell, Jr. Her soldier went to Germany without her, and his mother in Virginia stopped accepting her collect phone calls, and finally changed her phone number. She said she didn't think the baby was her son's child. Joy says she just didn't want to give up any part of her son's paycheck. Joy is living with her sister Nicky and her twin girls in a trailer park on the other side of town. There are dark circles under her eyes.

"Come see me sometime," she says, a cigarette dangling from between her hot pink lips. She gives me her phone number and I promise to call her, but I never do.

"Your mama called today," Aunt Faith says calmly, as if she is giving me the evening news, when I get home from school. She is sitting at the kitchen table folding and refolding a paper napkin.

"Where's she been all this time?" My voice sounds like an echo in an empty room.

"You want to know the truth, baby?" Aunt Faith asks, taking a deep breath, her eyes looking up toward the ceiling for the right place to begin.

I don't know if it is the right answer, but I whisper yes and try to prepare for where she is about to take me. I sit down in the chair beside her letting my books drop to the floor.

"Is she coming back now?" I ask, afraid to hear more, certain I will die from the fear spreading through the center of my body. I put my head down on the table and cover my face with my folded arms.

"She just finished a drug program, a good one in Michigan. This is the first time she's stayed anywhere longer than a week or two. I talked to the woman who runs the program and they said she's come a long way." She pauses to see if I am still listening. She squeezes my hand and releases it, then pushes away from the kitchen table. "When your mama was a little girl she would stay up late listening for trains so she could ride in her sleep. She went to sleep and woke up with traveling on her mind. Every morning she'd tell me and Merleen where she'd been and all the people she met in all the places she'd been in the night. She says she's tired of traveling now."

"Did she say when she was coming?" I ask.

"She say she won't disappoint you this time." Aunt Faith smiles a little but it is a sad mark her mouth makes.

This time I don't pack my bags and sit by the door. Still, I wait. Every day I expect the sound of her high heels coming up the front walk, but on Monday it's the postman, on Tuesday a neighbor lady returning a borrowed cake tray. By Friday I know Mama has missed another train. But at night I listen for the sound of her steps in the hallway. Every evening I sit on the bottom step, watching the front door, waiting for it to open. When Mama's promise begins to fade I decide I might like to do some traveling of my own.

*I* challenge my aunts daily to send me away. I cut classes, talk back to the teachers, don't turn in homework, curse the principal, smoke in the bathroom, and sometimes skip school altogether. I try to call my father but he is never home. My aunts try to call him in the hope that he will be able to do something about my attitude. After my third suspension from school, my aunts concede that I have won. They reach my father one rainy afternoon in April.

"We are too old for this," I hear Aunt Faith repeat over and over again. I am sitting on the stairs, my ears straining toward the kitchen where they are on the phone with my father. When Aunt Merleen calls me into the room her face is grim. She hands me the phone, and they sit like garden rocks at the kitchen table watching me. The phone is heavy in my hand, the receiver warm against my ear. I close my eyes and listen for something familiar.

"Mariah? Are you there?" His voice surprises me. It is gentle and concerned.

"I'm here," I say, quietly.

"It's your father. Baby, are you okay?"

I do not hesitate to test his love.

"Daddy, can I come live with you?" I ask, a cry forming in my throat.

"Yes. I want you to come. I'll send you a ticket tomorrow."

And just like that it is done. I am so happy I cry through the rest of our conversation, wiping my nose on my sleeve. When I turn to hand the phone back to my aunts they look sad. Suddenly I feel guilty for leaving them. We have come to depend on each other. Who will weed the garden when Aunt Merleen's arthritis flares up? Who will read the labels on Aunt Faith's medication bottles when her eyes are tired? They buy me books and fancy paper and pens to do what I love most and they love me, I know they love me. We have grown to love each other. But it is too late to take a step back. I run up the back stairs stopping to dance a few steps on the squeaky stair. I don't have much to pack. The things most precious to me are in the green suitcase. Then I remember Rosemary. Although the old cello has become my closest friend, it belongs to Aunt Faith's long-lost beau.

In the days before I leave we call a truce in the house. They don't want my father to think they haven't been taking good care of me. They don't lock me in at night anymore and I don't try to steal their car. They tell me more stories about when they were little girls in happier times. We even laugh a little. They insist on buying me some new clothes and shoes.

On the day of my departure me and Aunt Merleen walk down the hallway like we're on our way to prison. Aunt Faith taps me from behind on the shoulder. When I turn around she says, "You forgot something." She is holding Rosemary in a brand-new case. "Take care of her." I hug Aunt Faith so tight I squeeze tears out of us both. They promise to ship her to me on their way home. "She'll be waiting for you when you get there," Aunt Faith promises. Aunt Merleen brushes past us to go start the car.

On the way to the bus station Aunt Merleen cruises through a red light. Before Aunt Faith can say anything, Aunt Merleen says, "By the time you come back, this old woman will be coming to pick you up at the station."

"And when I do get behind the wheel you can bet I won't be running no red lights. I'm not going to be the second driver all my life. Shoot. I can drive, I just don't like to be rushed," Aunt Faith says, and we all laugh together as if it were any other Tuesday morning. Aunt Merleen turns into a gas station behind a line of cars.

"Why didn't you stop and get gas yesterday?" Aunt Faith complains as she dabs at sweat on the tip of her nose.

"Yesterday the line was twice as long. You watch my smoke—when the stock market crash for real folks are going to think we back in the Depression. Food prices high as it is. It's a good thing we got the garden," Aunt Merleen says.

"That's what that sorry president did. Inflation, recession . . . nothing but fancy new words for depression," Aunt Faith says, checking her watch.

"We'll be on time, don't worry," Aunt Merleen says loudly, inching up to the gas pump.

I'm not worried, just wondering if I have made the right decision. When we pass the train platform Mama and I walked on together, old feelings rise up from the bottom of my new shoes. I have been here so long the trains don't stop in this town anymore. Mama will travel into town another way if she ever comes back, but I'm not so hopeful of that anymore. I don't need to be now. At the bus station we sit together quietly watching the clock on the wall tick away the time. When my bus pulls in Aunt Faith starts to cry. They both hug me tight, tight, tight and remind me of all the things I must never forget: Be a lady . . . bedtime prayers . . . learn your lessons well.

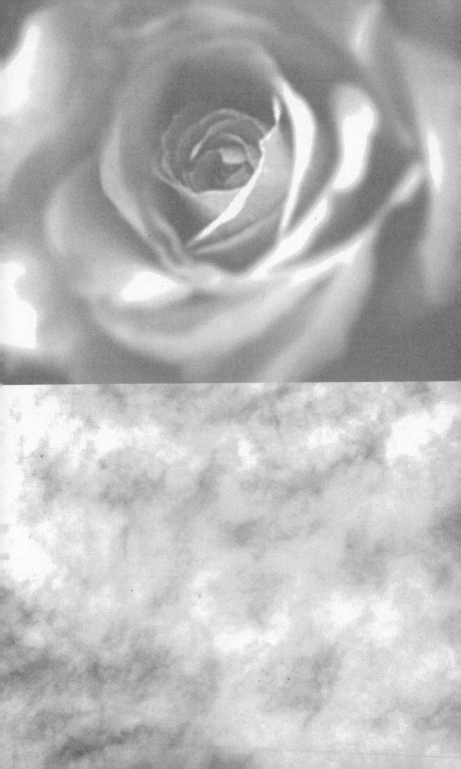

# NINE

*I* have a one-way bus ticket to Los Angeles that my father sent me. It is spring. I am fifteen years old and I feel grown, but I cry as the bus pulls away from the station. Maybe I'm afraid that all I can trust is over my left shoulder just out of sight behind me and all that I want is out of reach. For eight years I knew

I could depend on Aunt Faith and Aunt Merleen for food, clothes, and a safe place to dream. More than that, they have mothered me with a kind of love that I grew to know was solid as the faith of the congregation at the Macedonia Baptist Church. This thought makes me cry even harder. They have been nothing but kind to me when they didn't have to. At my school there are lots of girls living in foster homes who never see their own families. I want to turn the bus around, jump off and tell them that I love them, that I will do well in life so that their love won't have been wasted on me, but it is too late. We are crossing the bridge into Alabama.

"Nothing down the road is certain, that's the only thing for sure," Aunt Faith used to say.

My first travel companion is a young private. I can tell he is a private because of his tan uniform with the single shoulder stripe like the ones I remember from Kansas. He is short and bumpy with muscles. His large chest makes him look like he is pumped up with air. His chocolate skin looks smooth as a candy bar. I can tell he is going to want to talk because even though the bus is half empty he chooses the seat across the aisle from mine. He puts his bag overhead and settles into his seat. He starts clearing his throat and says, "Excuse me, but don't I know you?" Dimples dent his round cheeks and his eyes smile. We both know he has never seen me before. "You ever been to the NCO club out on the base?"

As soon as he asks my name I realize that I don't have to be Mariah Kin Santos, I don't have to be fifteen years old. I can be anybody I want to be.

"My name is Marie." If he thinks he met me in a club, he must think that I am older than fifteen.

"That's a pretty name. It fits you. Where you going, Marie?"

I like the way my new name sounds in his mouth, like a girl in a song.

"To L.A.," I say like I've been there.

"You don't need to go to L.A. They got enough stars out there without you. What you going out there for? You going to be a actress or something, I bet."

I smile, flattered by his attention, and he keeps talking. His name is Theotis and he has been discharged from the army because of a busted eardrum. He is on his way home to Mississippi. He talks about the Funkadelic concert he saw at the auditorium just before he left. I'd wanted to go, but Aunt Faith said she had to draw the line: "You are too young to be looking at grown men prancing around with rags on their heads, wearing diapers, cussing people out and talking about being funky. That noise they make could drive a deaf person crazy." Instead I listened to them on my little pink radio under the covers on the Album Hour at midnight on the night of the concert.

"Everybody at the concert was high. Even some of the security guards passed the peace pipe. It was funky." He laughs at his own jokes. At the first fifteen-minute rest stop he offers me a joint behind the Dumpsters at the Montgomery bus station. I've never smoked dope before, but Marie has, and I pretend that it's no big deal. I inhale as if it were a cigarette but the smoke is strong and makes me cough. Theotis puts his arm around me and tells me to take it easy. After a few seconds I begin to feel light and carefree. No more tears, no fears. Theotis buys us Cokes, ham sandwiches, and a handful of candy bars.

When we get back on the bus he sits in the seat next to me. After we eat I fall asleep with my head on his shoulder. By the time we cross the Mississippi state line he says has fallen in love with me. As an expression of his love he gives me a small plastic bag of pot from the enormous stash stuffed in his duffel bag. He teaches me how to roll a joint tight like a thin cigarette. He tells me all the things he wants to do in life. He is so sure of himself. Soon, he says, he will move to New Orleans to race cars.

"Black man don't have them kind of opportunities in Mississippi. I'm gonna do something with my life." I believe him.

"Marie, you're a pretty girl," he says when we get to his stop in Vicksburg. "You're gonna make somebody happy to be your man. I wish it was me. You be sweet." He kisses me quickly on the lips and I watch his wide back move down the aisle and out into the cool Mississippi night.

Theotis waves at me as the bus pulls away from his station. I put his address in my pocket and wonder who I'll be next.

Left alone with my thoughts I wonder if my mama when she started out from home ever looked out her traveling windows into Phenix City, Union Springs, Selma, Demopolis, and endless squares of southern fields. I wonder if this ride will be my last. I hope Los Angeles is the end of the line for me. I'm not like my mama in that way, I don't want to travel, I want to be somewhere.

Near midnight in Shreveport, Louisana, an older black woman with a shoebox full of fried chicken and half a loaf of sliced white bread squeezes her large body into the seat next to me. I can smell the fried chicken and the bread falls into my lap when she goes to put away her cardboard suitcase overhead. She sits down with a heavy sigh then yawns with her entire face.

"You look too young to be traveling by yourself, baby. Where you going?" she asks and offers me a piece of chicken. It is salty, greasy, and full of flavor. I have not tasted anything better in my life. We eat a whole chicken and all the bread in less than fifteen minutes. I tell her my name is Annette. "Annette is a sweet name," she says. Her name is Sister Lavine. She smiles a lot but she does not sound like a happy woman. She seems so alone in the world but she says Jesus satisfies all her needs. Sister Lavine is on her way to a Texas convention of missionaries going to Africa to claim souls for Christ. Because I am a good listener, she gives me a small white Bible and some pamphlets. She says she will pray for me. I try not to laugh when she hands me a piece of red cloth with zig-zag edges and tells me to put it in my wallet. She says it is a prayer cloth, one of only a dozen she has received from a television minister for a small donation. She assures me that if I am faithful in my prayers my wallet will stay full of money. I thank her and put it in my pocket next to three crisp twenties my aunts have given me in case of an emergency. I don't believe that the red cloth will multiply the money that is already there, but it can't hurt. I try to remember a ritual Mama had for making money appear in an envelope under the bed but I can't. I still believe in God even though it keeps me hoping for impossible things.

It is dawn when Sister Lavine gets off at her stop in Texas. I sit by myself for a long time. The small towns and cities sweep past the window. Time is thick and moves slowly in the heat. Swamps, rivers, dense woods, fields of corn, cotton, and soybeans stretch out alongside me and then are left behind with each passing mile. I feel as if I am shedding skin. My mind is muddy with thoughts. I see migrant workers picking vegetables in the hot sun and wonder if they speak Spanish and whether any of them might know Jesus Miguel Monteverde. I wish I was pregnant with his baby. I hope with all my heart that my father will love me like I would have loved my child.

It takes forever to cross Texas. It is hot and humid and the air conditioner on the bus is broken. When we arrive at the bus station in Dallas it is early evening just before sundown. We have a three-hour layover. I see signs for public showers and head straight for them. Inside the enormous ladies' room are a row of pay toilets and several large shower stalls with a metal box on the door that takes two dollars in coins. I dig out eight quarters, shove them in the narrow slot, and unlock the door. I put the green suitcase on a low metal bench that runs along one wall and I undress. I roll up my funky jeans and sweaty tee shirt, socks, and underwear and stuff them in a side pocket. I put my sneakers on top of the suitcase and walk several feet to the far side of the stall. Drawing the thin flowered plastic curtain, I turn the loose rusty knobs and a strong spray of water washes over me. The water is barely warm but it feels good. I unwrap a small bar of soap that smells like medicine and I wash away the dust of all the rest stops, cities, and towns. I rinse my body in cool water. When I am done I feel clean as a new nickel. I've forgotten that I have no towel. I shake myself to get as dry as possible, then use my shirt to soak up the remaining dampness. On the dry side of the stall I rub baby oil on my face and body and put on clean panties and a yellow stretch tube top that makes my breasts look big and a loose white jersey dress with spaghetti straps. I lace white roman sandals over my ankles. I want to look nice for my father. I brush my teeth and brush my hair out around my shoulders to dry naturally into a kind of flat afro with a part in the middle. It is the kind of hairstyle Aunt Faith would say makes me look like I went to sleep in the middle of combing it. Even though she is in Georgia I can hear her voice strong. I dig around in my bag for matches, then take a couple of drags off one of the joints Theotis gave me. It relaxes me immediately.

I sit in the waiting room. My bus connection to L. A. is two and a half hours away. I look around. There are lots of cowboys and Indians, Mexicans and old people in bright-colored clothes with loud voices and curious stares coming and going. A few old men pass me and ask for change with a quick upturned palm and hungry eyes. A wild-haired woman wearing an apron over what looks like three dresses of different lengths walks slowly in circles whispering to herself. I wonder what would make a person end up this way. Losing a job, a house, somebody you love? I wonder if my mother has a home someplace. I wonder if she is somewhere being crazy. I am lucky, I decide. Lucky to have somewhere to go, someone waiting for me when I get there.

My stomach growls. I am hungry, starving really, and I'm sick of eating vending machine sandwiches. An older man who looks like somebody's grandfather sits next to me. His skin is dark, tan, leathery, and looks creased like crumpled paper. A silver-haired cowboy.

"Where you going?" he asks and offers me a cigarette.

"L.A. I'm going to see my old man," I say. I take a cigarette from his pack.

"What's your name?"

"Tina," I say, because it sounds sexy and that's how I feel.

"Where you coming from, Tina?" he drawls slowly with a heavy Texan accent. He lights my cigarette, then runs his long fingers through his thick, curly hair. His dark eyes search my face for an answer.

"Georgia."

"I was in Georgia once. Did basic training down there."

"What's going on in Dallas?" I ask, noticing his long blue jean—covered legs that end in dusty black cowboy boots.

"If you was here for a few days I could show you around." He touches the small silver buttons at the neck of his blue jean shirt.

"I got a couple of hours to kill. Do you know anywhere around here I could get something to eat? I'm sick of bus station food."

"I know a good Mexican place not too far from here."

He looks me over, admiring my figure. I accept the compliment. My reason leaves me. I put the green suitcase in a large locker. We walk out into the parking lot to his car. He opens the door of his orange Pinto for me. He promises to get me back to the station on time. He is quiet as he speeds along the highway. It is getting dark.

"Is it far?" I am starting to get nervous.

"What?" he says, eyes on the road.

"The Mexican restaurant."

"No, it's not far."

He doesn't speak to me directly, just starts pointing out the names of buildings that define the Dallas skyline as we move past it. Finally, he turns off the highway onto a narrow dirt road and into a cornfield. Night is falling. He stops the car and turns to me.

"Why are we stopping out here?"

"Nice evening. Look at all them stars. You don't see stars like that in the city."

"I thought we were going to get some food."

"I'll get you something to eat later."

He reaches across the seat and tries to kiss me but I pull away. His voice is quiet, not menacing at all, but very serious.

"Take off your panties, Tina."

I don't want to be Tina anymore. I am scared, but try not to show it. I am cool.

"I think you better take me back to the bus station. I might miss my bus. My old man'll get worried if I'm late."

"Nothing to worry about out here," he says. "No one can hear you."

He shows me a knife he has pulled from under the seat. He draws the flat edge of the long blade slowly across my thigh.

I start to cry. "I don't want to," I say, gasping for air. I put my hand on the door handle and calculate my chances of outrunning him.

"Look, girlie, I don't want to hurt you, okay? Now take your panties off. I don't want to have to ask you again." He puts the knife away and lays both hands on my shoulders.

I rock my hips and slide my panties down my thighs and over my ankles. He takes them from me and tosses them on the dashboard. He makes me crawl over onto the back seat and lie down on my back. I can hear his belt unbuckling, his pants unzipping. He crawls over too and gets on top of me. He is heavy and I can hardly breathe. He smells fresh, like Irish Spring soap. The silver buttons on his shirt snap against the front of my dress. He rubs himself against me quickly, repeatedly, ignoring my cries. Before he can enter me he has come all over my dress. I look out the window and count stars in the country night sky. There is nothing blue in the landscape.

"Turn over. I won't come inside of you," he promises. He pushes my legs apart and presses himself into me, slower this time. I am dying.

*A is for apple . . . B is for boy . . . C is for car . . . D is for dog . . . E is for elevator . . . F is for far, far away. I am underwater. I am drowning, drowning, drowning. I scream, but no sound comes out of my mouth.*

When I open my eyes he is still there.
"I'm sorry," he says, weeping. "I'm so sorry."

*Be a lady . . . bedtime prayers . . . learn your lessons well . . .*

He strokes my face gently with the back of his big rough hand as if he really means it. He holds me to his chest rocking me as if I am a little girl. He looks like somebody's grandfather and he smells like Irish Spring soap. I want to scrape the surface of my skin with a knife, peeling away all the places he has touched me. Not just on the outside where his fingers have crawled like lice but inside of me where I can feel something cold, hard, and broken. I don't ever want to be touched again. I want to peel myself like an orange leaving only mangled pulp so no one will ever want to touch me again.

I am afraid to breathe wrapped in his strong arms. He finally releases his grip on me to light a cigarette. He sucks on the cigarette, blowing the sweet smoke out of the window away from my face. For a while it is quiet in the darkness except for the rhythm of our breathing.

"I didn't mean to hurt you. I'm sorry. I won't hurt you no more."

Silently he drives me back to the bus station. He writes his name and phone number on a piece of paper and says I should call him if I'm ever in trouble or if my father isn't nice to me. I get out of the car, walk into the station, get my green suitcase from the locker, and go back to the bathroom. In the shower I can't seem to scrub myself clean. I turn off the water and hear myself crying. I dry myself with paper towels and oil my bruised body. I put on a clean pair of panties and the funky jeans and damp tee shirt I'd had on earlier. I put on sneakers without socks. I roll up the soiled white dress and put it in the garbage can with the wet paper towels. I tear the piece of paper with his name and number on it into pieces and flush them down the toilet. I don't want to remember a thing but I do. Each digit is tattooed on my flesh. His name is chiseled onto my forehead. I look into the mirror above the sink to see if I am the same person.

*Mariah's face is there but she is dead in the field. I wash her face in the sink letting the water fill the basin and run over onto the floor. The sound of running water is soothing. I brush her hair into a ponytail. She smokes some dope and relaxes. After a while she doesn't feel anything. She's not even hungry anymore. It does not occur to her to tell anyone. It is all her fault.*

I call my father to tell him I have missed my bus. He says he will meet me at the bus station, that he will be wearing a white suit.

"Don't run off with a stranger," he jokes.

There is a stranger with a grandfather's face sleeping in my bones. Soon he will become the face in my nightmares I stab, but cannot kill, the sour taste on my tongue, the bad smell in the air, the sticky dampness on my thighs, permanent as indigo ink, rough as the teeth of a broken zipper biting my tender flesh. Soon I will separate from every little pain, each memory until it never happened. Marie, Annette, and Tina are dead.

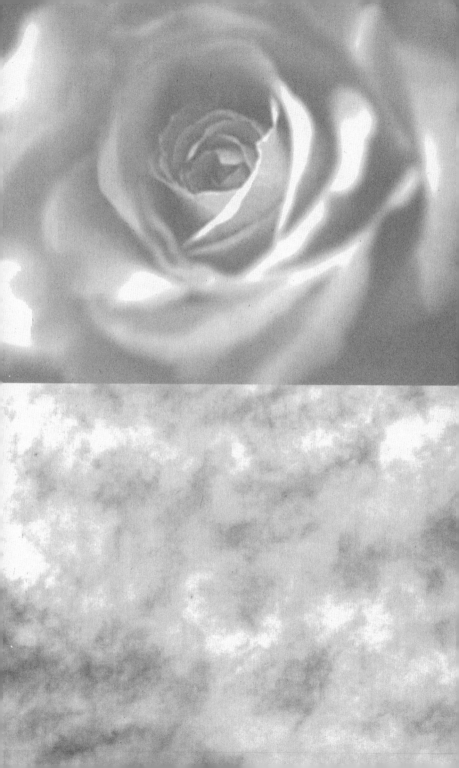

# TEN

$I$ am the last passenger to get off the bus in Los Angeles. My eyes are sensitive to the strong summer sunlight. When I step down I can feel the bruises on the inside of my thighs made by the man who held me down with his body in the back seat of a car, in a cornfield, in the middle of a starry night in

Texas. His whispers are like waves crashing in my ears. What if I had fought back ... if I had run ... or told someone. The sun warms my skin, but it feels strangely cold to be alive. I blink back tears wondering why the sun has to shine so brightly when there are dark thunderclouds on my insides. In many violent ways I have killed the man that hurt the body that seems to belong to some other girl. I have tied him to a telephone pole and allowed him to read my murderous thoughts as I drive a dump truck through his body. I have stabbed him with his own knife as he begs for mercy, I have hung him from an oak tree and shot holes the size of apples through his chest. I have lowered him into a pit of poisonous snakes, put a brain-eating bug into his ear and watched him lose his mind. Each time he begs for mercy, but I am not moved.

I feel so tired. I want my mother to rock me back to sleep. I want to call Aunt Faith and Aunt Merleen, but I am afraid of what they will think of me. They kept me safe for so long, I didn't know how dangerous life could be. I can't tell if I am coming or going, in which direction it is safe to travel. I don't know what to expect from one threatening mile to the next. This is the loneliest place I have ever been. I want to go home, to the place where I can I still expect to reach out and have my mother's hand to hold. Home, where words shaped to my tongue can be poured into my mother's mouth. There are fears no one else can soothe. Manhattan, Kansas, was not a perfect place, but it was safe and it was home. It was where I learned to dance as if the world had no underneath or up above, just in between and air. The "Manhattan, Kansas Dance," Mama called it, because it didn't matter how you danced, but that you danced as if it might be your last.

I take a deep breath. The breath I release makes me feel lightheaded. My misty eyes circle the bus station. I am looking for someone who looks like me. Someone bound to me by blood so I'll never feel lonely again, without hands to hold me. From the information counter, I see him before he sees me. Does my heart jump at the sight of him because he is my father or because he is my knight in a white linen suit? I've waited thousands of miles and sleepless nights for this moment and I am not disappointed. He is leaning against the pillars just outside the station, his arms crossed, head tilted to one side as if he were listening for the sound of my footsteps. His head is covered by a thick, dark wave of hair. His face is slim, the same color brown as mine, with large heavy-lidded eyes the color of burnt pennies, long, thick eyelashes like a woman's. Wide smiling mouth filled with large, white perfect teeth like a movie star's. He is the kind of handsome that makes men and women, young and old, even in California where everyone is beautiful, slow down to take a second look. He looks young, healthy, not like a father at all. I wonder if I am really his daughter. I wonder if the people around us will think he is my boyfriend. My heart is pounding in my chest.

I can feel the dope I smoked at the last rest stop starting to wear off. I have not come down since Dallas. The floating feeling distances me from the pain. As I walk toward him his eyes slowly sweep my body. He stares as if he can't believe his eyes. He speaks with a slight stutter as if he is afraid to push the next word forward into the air between us.

"Mariah. You're all grown up." He sounds surprised.

"Hey, Daddy," I say simply, my throat thick with southern inflections and the pain of a secret I can never tell. I wish I knew him well, I would fall into his arms and rain into his chest, forgetting everything I know about pain. Soon he will be everything to me.

"Call me Matisse," he says, unblinking.

We are awkward with each other, but when I see him I almost forget about Dallas. It seems so long ago. But my body is a ripe field of history. When he touches my face, my body reacts as if his hands are small fires putting themselves out on my skin. He hugs me so tight and so long that my breath is cut short, my body becomes rigid, but either he doesn't notice or he doesn't care. A new voice inside my head warns that touch can be dangerous.

He strokes my hair and smiles. He doesn't seem disappointed in me. I relax a little.

"Water," I say, taking a few steps away from him. "May I have some water, please?"

This distracts him. He lifts my bag and takes my hand. He leads me to a water fountain. He watches me drink as if we have forever. I wet my hands, press them to my face. My father is smiling. My father is carrying my bag. My father is taking me home. It is a miracle. A sure sign that everything will be all right now.

I am a wonder to him. So new. If I were his newborn baby daughter, he would undress me and count my fingers and toes, marvel at the texture of my skin, my newborn smell, the minute measure of my nose and lips so much like his. With reverence, he would kiss and fondle my tiny face, neck, hands, and feet. He would be astonished by the miracle of my birth, a perfect baby girl. But I am a woman. I have come to him broken and impressed by the world. My lips are full of grown-up kisses, my mind full of grown up thoughts. My limbs marked by grown-up bruises. I have a woman's body.

Matisse drives the old gray Renault fast on the freeway. The wind is white noise in my ears. We are shy with each other, stealing glances when we think the other isn't looking. There is no more talking. He hums. I look out the window at the palm trees and blue sky, feel the sun on my face, taste the smog. I take out the cigarettes given to me by the man who hurt me and crush the red and white package in my fist. I know that I will be killing the memory of that night one minute at a time for the rest of my life. I throw the pack viciously out the window, onto the freeway.

"Why did you do that?" Matisse looks over at me, annoyed.

"I need to quit," I answer mechanically. I look at the road ahead of us, my mind far in the distance, as far from Texas as I can go without dying.

"We're off to a good start," he says, a hint of sarcasm in his voice.

My father's first-floor apartment is small, sparsely furnished. A one-bedroom. He tells me that I am to sleep in the living room on the denim-covered daybed. A picture window veiled in sheer white curtains looks out onto a busy strip of apartment complexes and fast food restaurants in West Hollywood. The off-white walls are covered with large, richly colored paintings of blue trees with blurry figures running in the dark. A half-dead ficus tree weeps in the corner next to the tv and stereo. This is my new home. I will make myself fit my new life. I am near tears when I see Rosemary leaning against the wall, waiting for me. I want to open her up, hold her close, and let her heal me. Later when we are alone, I will take medicine from her body, wrap us both in sweet, blue music and dreams.

Matisse drops my bags on the floor by the daybed and shows me into the dining room, where a card table and three chairs crowd the room. Beyond it is a small kitchen with spotless stainless steel appliances. It smells like burnt meat and vinegar. We circle back to the living room and continue down the hall, past a tiny pink bathroom. At the end of the hall is his bedroom, its king-sized bed made up with crisp white linens and half a dozen plump white pillows. It looks like an island. Suddenly I am overcome with fatigue and feel as though I could sleep for days. I sit down on the bed and look up at him, his image wavering like a flag in front of the open venetian blinds. The light is too bright.

"Can I lay down here?" I ask him, leaning back onto the big, white island of his bed, closing my eyes.

"Sure. I've got to go out for a little while. There's food in the fridge and sodas too." He closes the blinds and turns on the air conditioner.

He bends down and unties my sneakers, slipping them off carefully along with my socks. I feel like a little girl, pampered and tended to as if only my needs matter.

"Get comfortable. Sleep here for a while. You can unpack later." His voice is a distant whisper. I curl my body into a ball and fall into a deep sleep. In my first Hollywood dream the weather is perfect.

When I wake up it is dark and I am alone on the white island. I feel around until I find the switch on the lamp by the bed. I feel dizzy, my head spins as invisible ants crawl up my legs. I stare at the phone wondering if I should call home. With my finger I draw the word onto the stark white wall above my father's bed as if to make it so. *Home.* After a while I lie down in the dark again, but no dreams comfort me.

When the phone rings I am so startled I jump up, feet to the floor, arm reaching for something solid. I knock a lamp over onto the floor. I'm not sure what to do. Maybe my mother calls him. What if she is the voice on the phone? What will I say? How can I make words that will sew us back together again? The phone rings a dozen times, stops, then rings again. Finally I pick up the receiver.

"Hello," I say through a fog of weariness.

"Why didn't you pick up the phone the first time we called?" Aunt Merleen asks impatiently.

"I wasn't sure if I should answer his phone." I sit up in the bed and count the squares on the sliding doors of my father's closet. What I want to say is, I miss you, but it does not come out of my mouth.

"Well, where is he?" Aunt Faith asks nervously on the other line.

"He went out." I want to explain to them how tired I am.

"He left you there all by yourself?" Aunt Merleen is furious.

"He'll be back." I shout to calm them.

There is a small silence in which Aunt Merleen famously sucks her teeth.

"You tell him to call us tomorrow. We just wanted to check on you, make sure you got there all right." There is a wound opening in Aunt Faith's voice.

"I'm all right. Everything is okay." I am a little softer.

"Don't tell him about that little piece of money we give you. You call us if you want to come home." Their voices blend into one.

"Yes ma'am," I say, opening a small box of pain. They remind me that I have left something precious with them. I have two homes now. "Thank you," I remember to be a lady. They have taught me well. I have taught myself not to wear my feelings on the outside, so I try not to reveal how much I miss the ordinariness of our everydays together.

When Matisse returns hours later I am sitting on the day bed in the living room watching tv. I have never watched so many hours of tv in a row and I am fascinated even by the commercials. He sits down beside me and hugs me like it is the first time.

"How's my baby girl? Did you sleep okay?" he asks, his arm tight around my shoulders.

"Fine," I answer, feeling a wall of glass rise up around my fear. It is not true, all the happiness I imagined would be in this moment has not arrived, but I think *fine* is what he wants to hear. So I say this to reassure him. I want to feel like a family, whatever that means. Comfortable, like I belong, like we belong together. I am stiff in his arms, I do not know him yet.

"Fine. Everything is fine," I repeat like a prayer.

But nothing is ever the same. The sound of rain makes me cry, so does the mention of corn, the smell of Irish Spring soap, the color orange, and the taste of Mexican food. I barely speak above a whisper. I could not scream if I tried and I have tried, but only invisible sounds escape my bruised lips.

"You're so quiet," my father says across the dining room table during our first family dinner.

I pick the slices of pepperoni off the top of my wedge of pizza and stack them on the edge of the paper plate.

"Do you want something else to eat?"

"I'm not so hungry," I say, counting the slices of meat on my plate.

"Tomorrow we'll go to Redondo Beach. Do you like seafood?"

"It's okay," I answer, rearranging the pepperoni into a pyramid.

"Just tell me what you like. Anything. What did they feed you down south to make you so quiet, cornbread and possum parts?" He laughs and collects our paper plates. On his way to the kitchen he runs his hands across my shoulders. He is trying so hard to love me, but he does not understand the deep sadness that flavors every meal for me.

The first time I take a shower in the pink-tiled bathroom I find myself humming under the hot spray of water. So I don't hear my father enter the room, I only see the shadow of his frame at the sink, then the sound of running water. I open my mouth and slam my naked body into a corner of the shower trying to cover myself.

"I'll be out of here in a second," he says casually, and begins brushing his teeth. I feel as if a war has broken out inside the tight, steamy room. I am trembling, holding my breath and my body against the wall. The tiles are cold against my back, the grooves imprint crosses onto my flesh. I am afraid he will slide open the frosted glass door and make marks on me I'll have to erase. But he doesn't. He only brushes his teeth, washes his face and hands. After what seems like an hour he says, *"Hasta luego."* Then he leaves me alone in the bathroom.

I don't shower much when my father is home, neglect to bathe sometimes for days which he complains about, but I don't care.

We have been together for two weeks now. I keep my distance, but I want to know everything about him. He doesn't say much and I don't know how to scratch the surface of his answers.

"Do we have a family?" I ask after we have eaten our supper of take-out Chinese food.

He wipes his mouth delicately, a gesture that seems to mean he is gathering up his courage to say something he doesn't want to. He gets up from the dining room table and goes to stand by the window that looks down on the alley behind the apartment. He talks to the windowpane.

"They live in Seattle. My dad lives with your aunt Corrina and her family. I haven't seen them for years. Not since Mother died." His voice cracks on the word *Mother*.

"Why not?" I am disappointed. In my fantasies of life with my father I imagined a large extended family with dozens of cousins and family reunions by the beach. Brothers and sisters to spoil me and remind me that I will never be alone in the world.

"I'm sort of the black sheep of the family. Dad was a big musician back in the forties. He played bass in a jazz band, so you got your musical talent honest."

"Did he teach you how to play?" I ask.

"He wasn't around enough to teach me much besides how to read train schedules so I could figure out when he was coming home. Dad traveled with the band and Mother stayed at home to look after us. They wanted their children to be practical. Dad was the one really, he wanted us to be professional people, respectable. He thought we would make him look good if we became doctors or teachers or engineers. Mother just wanted us to be happy. I'm a great disappointment to him." I can't see my father's face but his voice is low and heavy.

"What did you want to be?" I ask. He does not hesitate.

"I didn't want to be anything. I just wanted to paint." He turns around to face me his arms folded across his chest.

"What do you want to do with your life?" he asks. I don't know if I can trust him. I open my mouth to speak but it sounds ridiculous. Play the cello, write, travel by airplane. Those are things I want to do, not things I believe I can get a job doing. I'm not sure if that's what he means.

"I don't know yet." I stuff my mouth with another plastic fork full of fried rice before he asks another question.

He tells me that my aunt Corinna is an architect. Her husband is a successful real-estate agent and they have two young daughters.

"I quit school when I was seventeen. I wanted to be an artist. I came to San Francisco around 1955. I lived on the streets a while. Nothing glamorous about that. To make money, I got work on the docks loading freight on ships, then I started painting houses with a buddy of mine. I taught myself how to paint portraits. Your mother was one of my first models." He pauses and looks me in the eye. "Do you know the French artist Matisse?"

I nod yes.

"I took the name Matisse because I had to be somebody new, not Joe El's little boy." He is quiet for a while, ripping his paper napkin to pieces.

"I want to make words so delicious that people will want to eat them," I say, deciding to trust him after all. We both laugh. It sounds ridiculous, but he takes me seriously.

"Anything is possible." He looks down into the alley again as if remembering his own delicious dreams.

"There was a poem I found. You sent it to my mother," I say, breaking the silence.

"Coral said she used to lick the ink from my letters till her tongue turned blue so that you could memorize the poems in her belly. Your mother was truly an invention. Do you remember?"

I lick my lips as if I can taste the love between them. Taste the poems she fed me in her womb so long ago. I shake my head no, wishing that I did.

"I didn't have much to offer Coral when we met but love, poems, and a handful of paintings. I didn't believe it was enough then. I wish it hadn't mattered, but I was young and my father's son. I wanted to take care of her, like a man is supposed to take care of the woman he loves, but I didn't think I could do that and be an artist too. I couldn't let a woman take care of me, but she offered."

I want him to tell me more. He comes over to the table and pulls up a chair next to mine. He lays his head on the table and continues to talk.

"After she left I painted pictures of her every day. Our first night together I woke up and she was circling the bed, naked in the moonlight, reciting that poem *'Un río de promesas . . .'* She found a collection of Nicolás Guillén poems in a bookstore on La Brea. She wanted to learn Spanish. She was so beautiful."

"She's not dead."

"But she's not here."

"Maybe she'll come back to us." I pat him on his back to comfort him. He leans his face into the circle of his arms, sighing.

"Maybe. She opened me up in the most unexpected ways like she had a razor digging the realness out of me." He raises his head and looks at me. "Your mother was in L.A. training at the hospital. She was thinking about quitting the army and traveling around for a while. She was like me in that way, neither of us wanted an ordinary life."

I take his hand and hold it until the the room is so dark it feels like midnight. We are beginning to feel a little like family.


We live like bachelors. When school starts in September, he drops me off at the bus stop each weekday morning and goes to paint houses in the valley. At night he goes to his studio. At school the kids are black and white, Asian and Hispanic, well dressed and smart. Most of the girls ignore me and the boys give me searching looks I don't return. I talk different, my clothes are different, and I don't fit in here either.

While taking a forbidden smoke in the bathroom at lunch, I am invited into a conversation two girls are having about Muhammad Ali's upcoming fight with George Foreman. I don't know much about boxing but we each agree that Ali is the cutest and the greatest boxer in the world. I have a dream where Muhammad Ali teaches me how to box, then gives me kissing lessons as a bonus. Candy and Bertine are the only girls who speak to me between classes and we always meet to smoke in the morning before classes. They call me Santos and teach me how to curse in Spanish. Sometimes they speak to each other in Spanish, sometimes we don't talk at all.

After school I turn on the tv for company and leave it on all evening, sometimes reading and doing my homework with the sound turned down. I watch tv to educate myself. I learn how to dance watching "Soul Train," about relationships from "The Young and the Restless," how black families make jokes out of their lives from "The Jeffersons," "Good Times," and "Sanford and Son." I learn about the law from "Police Woman" and the importance of friendship from "Laverne and Shirley." I check out diction tapes from the library and practice speaking out loud to erase my southern accent so when I raise my hand to speak in class my teachers will understand me. Sometimes I play my cello until Matisse comes home so late Johnny Carson is almost over. Rosemary is a big comfort to me in all the hours I spend alone. We make sounds that massage my lungs, my heart, the insides of my thighs. I miss the poetry of southern words in my mouth so I plant a few in the ficus tree and water them tenderly . . . *yonder ways . . . sweet potato pie . . . cut the monkey . . .* and always I plant *sweet . . . blue . . . music . . . Mama.* Soon the plant begins to grow, a bit sideways and very slowly, but I see growth and all the words I love in each green veined leaf.

Mostly Matisse cooks for himself because his doctor says that he should watch his diet since his heart attack last year. He was in a Chinese restaurant working on a wall mural when he passed out. He woke up in the hospital. Now he broils steaks, bakes potatoes, and tosses green salads with rice vinegar dressing almost every day. Sometimes he brings home take-out for me. I have alphabetized the take-out menus for over twenty restaurants within a five-mile radius. Although he is careful about what he eats, he encourages me to experiment with food. At first I refuse to eat raw fish even though it costs over twenty dollars a plate. But he bribes me with promises of trips to the ocean, movies at the mall, and shopping in Japan town. I learn to like sushi, California rolls, steamed bok choy, Thai tea with condensed milk, coconut soup with lemongrass, spanakopita, and pizza with bacon and pineapple slices. I like these new tastes and sometimes I close my eyes and pick something on a menu I have never tried.

In the beginning I am afraid when he goes out at night. There are no pink lights or soft music on the radio to soothe me. No gentle snoring and late-night coughs drifting from the other room to let me know I am not alone. What if the man who chases me in my dreams comes back again? What if I can't kill him with a knife? What if he doesn't bleed?

"I can't sleep when I'm here by myself," I say, standing in the doorway to the bathroom watching him shave in the mirror.

"Did you try counting sheep?" He strokes at the white lather underneath his chin delicately.

"They're too noisy." I shift from one foot to the other pulling at the hem of Mama's pink slip.

"Did you try turning off the tv and closing your eyes?" He lets the hot water run, fogging up the mirror.

"I'm serious. I've been falling asleep in class. Can't you stay home tonight, please?"

"I can't, not tonight." He wets a white hand towel and presses the moist heat against his face.

I feel a sharp pain of jealousy. He slaps on some aftershave. Vetiver. It smells like fresh lime and musk. It excites me. Sometimes I rub a little on my finger at night and inhale it until I fall asleep. I want to touch my father's face, press my fingers to his lips to test their softness, see how much they feel like mine. I wonder how my mother felt when she kissed him, if she felt an earthquake move through her body.

Suddenly my father seems to notice that I'm wearing my mother's slip. He reaches over and touches the satin fabric at my waist. My body jerks away as if pricked by a hot needle. I step backward into the doorway, out of his reach.

"You look so much like your mother," he says, eyes dreamy, remembering. "It's a little tight, isn't it?" He looks away. We are both made aware of our mistake. I remember to wear a tee shirt over the slip no matter how hot it gets. A few of the seams have split since my body has begun to fill out.

"Here, take one of these." He gives me a small, yellow pill from a bottle in the medicine cabinet. "Take another half if the Sandman doesn't come."

"What is it?" I ask.

"Valium. It'll help you relax." He finishes dressing in a pale amber silk suit and he leaves me in the apartment alone. It is Friday night. Back home we three ate together every night. I would have a piano lesson after supper while Aunt Merleen sat in her chair reading the newspaper. My lesson done, I would have a piece of homemade pie or cake and afterward wash the dishes while Aunt Faith put the food away. Later I would thread needles for Aunt Faith or read out loud to them. In summertime we would sit on the screened porch and watch Aunt Merleen's flowers grow. I wonder what real families with a mother, father, brothers, and sisters do on Friday evenings. I wonder if they do things or just sit around loving each other.

I lock up after Matisse leaves and get a glass of water from the kitchen. I swallow one of the yellow pills and lie on my bed with the light on. I remember about a dozen of Mama's words before I fall asleep.

*Urged by my fingers, the trembling begins in the deepest part of me and continues until all the blue windows of my imagination are broken and my body is free and floating toward the ceiling. My body rises in anticipation of music. The sweet trembling begins again, in the deepest part of me. My fingers press into the wet crease and a salsa floats through my open window.*

ELEVEN

*I* wake up in the dark to the sound of glass breaking. Still sleepy, on unsteady feet, I run to Matisse's bedroom, but he isn't there. The floor is moving, shaking. Pictures fall off the wall. I can't move fast enough. I forget everything I am supposed to remember during an earthquake. I slide back the panel to the closet in his bedroom and sit there among his clothes and shoes until everything is still. I hear a chaotic symphony of burglar alarms, sirens, and fire alarms. Before I can get out of the closet, a huge steel-gray film projector and round metal film boxes fall from the top shelf at my feet.

It takes me a while to figure it out, but I set up the projector. It looks like the one in my biology class that shows us how frogs reproduce. I sit on my father's bed mesmerized. Black and white images flicker on the white wall above the bed. There is a carnival of naked bodies in countless sexual combinations draped over the furniture in a suburban living room. The images excite and terrify me at the same time.

*There is a sweet trembling in the deepest part of me . . .*

I put my hand inside my pajamas and make myself come quickly and quietly. I put the projector and the films back on the shelf in the closet. It is so quiet I can hear the water from the leaky faucet in the bathroom dripping with loud pings into the sink.

In the closet his white suit sags on its hanger. I step back inside and slide the doors shut. In the dark I feel the rough texture of the linen suit, let my fingers caress the cool buttons, the seams, the insides of silk-lined pockets. I wrap the arms around my shoulders and bury my face in the lapels. It smells so much like him. I sniff the crotch of his pants. I huddle in a corner of the closet and feel for his shoes. Soft leather shoes, handmade in Italy. I take a deep breath of his footprints and I sigh.

His underwear, at least a dozen pair, all white, is folded neatly in the second drawer of the mahogany bureau at the foot of his bed. I am overwhelmed with feelings I do not understand. I give in. I take off my clothes, one piece at a time before a trinity of mirrors. I strip slowly and deliberately.

When I am naked I look at my body with his eyes. For hours it seems I stare at my body in the mirrors and then, finally, something happens. I begin to see his hands caressing my shoulders from behind. I can't take my eyes away from his hands. They feel the weight of my breasts, graze my nipples, trace the curve of my waist down to my thighs, then open the lips between my legs. I am paralyzed with fear, longing, and desire. And then just as suddenly as they appeared his hands are gone. I close my eyes, then open them very slowly, but they do not reappear. I am still alone.

My father's boxer shorts are cool and fit loosely over my thighs, snug at the waist. The undershirt is tight and binds my breasts almost flat against my chest. I ease the silk socks over my feet and the rough linen over my thighs. The white shirt is crisp and buttons smoothly. I find a pair of gold cufflinks. The tie I slip over my head and knot easily, just the way he has shown me. I attach the yellow silk suspenders and snap them with my thumbs. The jacket is comfortable and loose. The shoes fit like a dream.

I look at the me in the mirror and I am pleased. Aunt Merleen must have known how well they would suit me when she gave me my boy's clothes so long ago. I do not feel vulnerable in these clothes. I feel powerful, strong, and aroused. I strut and stroll, pose and profile past the mirrors. I wander around the house wearing my father's clothes until daybreak.

I undress again, hanging my father's suit back where it belongs. I keep the white shirt on to protect me in my sleep. I wash down two Valiums with a mouthful of water. I hope that my father is safe and that he comes home soon. I wonder if the earth has opened up and swallowed half the city. I watch tv for awhile to make sure. I am afraid to sleep near the picture window in the living room which could shake and shatter my sleep. I go into in my father's bedroom, lay down to sleep in his king-sized bed, between the cool white cotton sheets. It seems as if I sleep, dreamless, for days. When I wake up my father is standing by the bed watching me.

"Are you okay?" he asks.

"I'm fine . . . I forgot what to do in an earthquake." I can barely keep my eyes open.

"Why are you wearing my shirt?" He sits down on the bed.

"I forgot . . . I'm awake . . . I'm okay." I know I am not making sense. My brain is soupy.

"Go back to sleep, baby. You must be tired. You don't have to go to school today unless you want to," he says. "And take my dress shirt to the cleaners when you get up." He smiles down at me.

"I was so scared," I mumble, then close my eyes thankfully.

He covers my shoulders with the sheet and kisses my forehead. I sink back into a deep sleep. When I wake up it's lunchtime. He orders a large pizza, which we eat on the living-room floor.

Matisse is stretched out on the floor, his head propped against his hand. His loose jeans and gray tee shirt are spotted with bright orange paint.

"I got a job painting a backyard swing set. It'll pay for pizza this week." He opens the box and passes me another slice of thin crust pepperoni with artichoke hearts. He acts as if it is any other Monday.

"That was a pretty big earthquake last night," I say, shifting my back against the unmade daybed.

"It was only a four point two, not much damage." He sprinkles red pepper flakes on his slice.

"Except to my nerves." The pizza tastes funny, too salty. I make a face when I discover that there are anchovies under the pepperoni.

"Most people sleep right through them."

I wonder if I will sleep through the next one.

"How many Valium did you take last night?"

"Two or three . . . I don't remember. I was scared."

"Be careful. One should be enough to help you get to sleep." He reaches over and rubs his hand roughly over my uncombed hair.

"Your aunt Corinna called a few days ago. She and her girls want to meet you. Do you want to go up to Seattle for a few days? Maybe you could go shopping or something." He picks the anchovies off my plate and pops them into his mouth.

"I hate shopping." My response is quick and sharp.

"I just thought you might want to do some girl things." He pretends not to notice the change in my mood. I don't feel ready to share him or to travel yet. I want to know him more.

"Do you want to go? Do you miss your father?" I ask.

"I didn't used to think about it much." I don't believe him. "I didn't realize how lonely I was until you came."

"I was lonely too."

"I won't leave you," he says. I try to believe him, some part of me does.

He smiles at me and kisses the back of my hand. Blood rushes to my face. I take his hand and rub it against my face like an affectionate cat. He suddenly pulls away from me and stands up. I watch his back as he walks with weighted shoulders into his bedroom and shuts the door. I lie on the floor a long time, thinking about the movies in my father's closet. I begin to notice how his body moves in his clothes. I wonder what I would look like in a suit of my own.

Some mornings I test my father.

"I don't feel so good," I say, making my voice weak and low.

"What's the matter?"

"My head hurts."

"Let me take your temperature." He puts the thermometer under my tongue and rests his hand on my forehead. I keep my eyes closed and focus on the warm touch of his hand. Sometimes I like it when he touches me, holds my hand or holds me in the curve of his arms. I feel like his little girl. I invent illnesses and canceled classes and look forward to days off with him. When I pretend to be vaguely ill he pampers me, buys me ginger ale, and stays home holding my hand even after he knows I am not sick. I think he secretly likes the days we play hooky together.

Sometimes he tells me stories about when he was Joe El's little boy.

"My father was so proud of me. When I was around four or five he would take me with him to gigs sometimes. He would sit me on top of pianos in smoky bars and let me sip from his bottomless glasses of scotch. Joe El would tell anybody who would listen that his son was going to be a rich lawyer someday. I broke my daddy's heart."

When Matisse tells stories about his father I can tell it makes him sad. When he's sad he goes to his studio to paint and I am left behind. Sometimes I watch his sex movies while holding Rosemary, my sweet cello, in my arms, plucking out a soundtrack.

I take one Valium every night my father leaves me alone in the apartment, sometimes two.

*O*ne day my father begins teaching me how to see.

"What color is the grass?" he asks as we walk arm in arm through Griffith Park at dusk.

"Green," I am savoring the closeness of him.

"What kind of green?" He gives my arm a light squeeze.

I dig deeper into my vocabulary for a word to match the color of evening light on dew-dampened grass. "Emerald." He rewards me with a kiss on my neck just beneath my ear. The kiss makes my toes tingle, makes the place on my neck burn.

"Look at the observatory. See how the light curves."

I follow the arc of light his fingers trace in the darkening sky.

"Now bend over and look at it upside down between your legs."

I do as he tells me and the world is changed. Blood rushes to my head, and I start laughing so hard I fall on the ground. Matisse helps me up and puts his arms around me in a tight hug as if he has almost lost me.

"Listen to the night," he says leaning over the railing of the observatory into the city spread out before us like diamonds on a plate. The wind chills me, opens up a place inside of me that remembers the cool flat blade across my thighs, remembers the stillness of night in a Texas cornfield. I close my eyes and I can hear blue night music as if a single sound has wrapped its arms around me. It is cold and I am crying in my father's arms. He holds me as if I am his alone and all the nights are ours.

"It's all right. Everything will be okay. Daddy's here." He doesn't ask me why I'm crying.

Matisse teaches me perspective, to look at objects from all sides before assigning them value. When we look at paintings in the Museum of Contemporary Art he asks me if I like a particular piece, then he asks me why. He makes me name my feelings. I look at the world with the new eyes Matisse has given me. I am so drunk from the things he pours into my mind, I begin to forget things.

*I* call my aunts every Sunday evening from the phone on the kitchen wall. I sit at the card table in the dining room with the cord wrapped around my arm. Every Sunday Aunt Faith asks me the same question.

"Mariah, have you found a church to go to?"

"Not yet," I answer, tightening the cord around my finger.

Aunt Merleen, less concerned with my soul, asks, "Is he treating you all right?" Her voice is tight and unnatural.

"Fine. Everything is fine," is what I answer every time. I realize that when I lived with them, someone was always near whether or not we were speaking to each other and I grew to depend on that. I ache for the smell of them, the closeness of their bodies on either side of me during Sunday church service. I hear concern in their questions, a small fear in the moment before I answer them that wonders if we have all made a big mistake.

I wonder what my aunts have told my father about me, about the trouble I caused them in the end, because after a few weeks he wants to know everything:

*When I have my period.* Every twenty-two days like clockwork. My first weeks in L.A. I punched myself in the stomach several times a day until thick, dark clots of blood passed between my legs and not a gray-haired baby with a grandfather's face.

*Which teachers I like.* Mrs. Oyama, the geography teacher, is pretty and smiles at me a lot. She has smoke-colored almond-shaped eyes like my mother's that disappear when she smiles. After class I bring her small presents—a perfect orange, an avocado, a bowl of lemons, and, one day, a yellow rose.

*Who I hang out with at school.* Candy and Bertine because they both have heavy accents and don't make fun of mine. Candy is from Nicaragua and Bertine from East L.A. They smoke cigarettes with me in the bathroom before school starts, sometimes talking to each other in Spanish as if I am not there. They talk about the cute boys on the basketball team, who is the best kisser, who is the most aggressive in the back seat of a car. I only listen to these conversations. I am not interested in being in the back seat of a car with a boy. Sometimes I think about kissing Bertine but I do not say this. I think about how Joy and I kissed and it makes me want to be grown up so I can kiss whomever I want. The smell of the sweaty boys who pass me in the halls makes me feel the urge to kill. I have never been to a basketball game because they are usually in the afternoons and evenings after school, and my father says that I must come home each afternoon and lock the door behind me and not open it for anyone because it is dangerous in L.A. Anyone could be in a gang, he says. My father wants me to bring my friends home so he can check them out, but I want to keep some things to myself. It is not long before Candy and Bertine are no longer my friends.

One morning after smoking a cigarette in the bathroom Candy pulls a cigar box from her book bag.

"My brother just came back from Hawaii on the Big Island." She opens the box to reveal a plastic bag full of what she tells us is Kona Gold.

"Your brother gave you all that?" Bertine asks and whistles through the gap in her front teeth in amazement.

"No, *pendeja!* He had a suitcase full of it. He won't miss this."

Candy puts the box on the window ledge and pulls out a pack of rolling papers. She teaches us how to roll a joint. It looks easy in her quick brown fingers. Before we can light up we hear someone in one of the stalls. Bertine takes the one rolled joint and Candy stuffs the rest of the pot in her book bag. We stroll out of the bathroom and head for our first classes.

"Later," I say.

"Later," they repeat in unison. Later we will smoke a joint of Hawaiian dope and float through the rest of our lives.

I am sitting in Mrs. Oyama's geography class not two hours later when the vice principal, Mr. Martinez, walks into the room and up to Mrs. Oyama's desk. They whisper together briefly, then she calls my name.

"Mariah Santos, please take your books and go with Mr. Martinez." She gives me a hard look. I gather my things and follow him down the hall. My heart is in my mouth. Mr. Martinez doesn't speak to me. I don't know what is happening. In the principal's waiting room I see Candy and Bertine slumped in chairs across the room from each other. They both cut me cold with their looks as I walk past them. A police officer is sitting between them flipping through a magazine. I am led into the principal's office where two police officers, one male and one female, are waiting for me.

"Candela Vega and Bertine Ramos are being expelled. Do you know why?" the vice principal asks me. I act uninterested in whatever the answer may be.

"You will be expelled too if we find that you've been involved in any criminal drug activites." They search my bag and ask me to detail my movements since I arrived at school that morning. I repeat several times that I smoked a cigarette in the bathroom with Candy and Bertine knowing that I was breaking the rules but, no, I don't know anything about drugs. I do know from watching tv movies that a confession could be put in my record and that if there is no evidence or eyewitness they have no case, and besides we are minors; I know my rights. After two hours, I sign a statement. I am told that I've been suspended for three days and that I will only be allowed to return to school with a signed letter from a parent. I collect my books and walk outside. Candy and Bertine are being led away by the police. When I try to call them later at home I am told that they are not allowed to talk to me.

After this incident Mrs. Oyama takes a special interest in me. Because I have missed an important exam she tells me that I must come to her classroom during study hall to catch up. She seems sincere in her concern. I notice her eyes and the color of her dress and the fragrant smell of jasmine when she passes me. I watch her gestures and they seem familiar. She is always dropping things and I am always picking them up so that I can see the smoke in her eyes, the smile that seems to be just for me.

He likes to think I tell him everything, but I don't. I keep secrets.

*W*ithout friends the days pass like mud. Candy and Bertine are expelled from school and put on probation. I am given a lecture on the dangers of drugs. When I get home, Matisse is packing a suitcase. He is conveniently going to New Mexico for a few days to help paint the house of a friend he owes a favor.

"Are you sure you won't be afraid here by yourself?"

"I'll be fine." I have made sure there is an adequate supply of the little yellow pills in the medicine cabinet.

"Is there anything you need? Anything I can do before I go?" he practically begs.

"Take me with you."

"Not this time." He looks up from his packing and gives me a wink.

I put up a tough front, but deep down I wonder if he'll come back. I spend the weekend watching tv, ordering Chinese food, and charging it to Matisse's American Express card. My father drives me everywhere. The only place I have walked to from the apartment is the hot dog stand on the corner and the dry cleaners two doors down. My world here is inside. I call Bertine, but her sister answers the phone and says she is in North Dakota. After hours of practice I sign my father's name to the letter describing my suspension from school and fold it neatly back into the envelope addressed to the vice principal. When I am not watching tv, I am sleeping. Two Valiums and a sip of mineral water knock me out cold.

My first day back, in English class, Mr. O'Farrell talks about the history of words. He explains that the oldest known form of writing is called hieroglyphics. The word itself means sacred carving. He tells us how the Rosetta Stone was found in 1799 by members of Napoleon's expedition to Egypt and translated by a French linguist in 1822. Mr. O'Farrell makes history sound like a place you'd like to live.

Suddenly I can't seem to focus on the page. I am haunted by the ink beneath my fingernails. My palms itch. Between classes I steal a thick, black magic marker, red poster paint, and pink chalk from the art supply closet. I knot my dress at my waist and crawl along on my bare knees as I write pink powdered words onto the sidewalk and thick black words onto the bottom of the wall leading to the lunchroom. I write from right to left, then left to right, like a snake moving through still water. The words are sacred, unreadable, unspeakable, but necessary. I understand them, but I will not translate them. I paint the word *mother* in red. The only word I cannot figure out. The word that will not vanish. The hall monitor, a skinny Mexican girl with long black braids and a pink beret on her head, holds a pencil and pad in her hands to take the names of hall loiterers, loud talkers, and offenders. When she sees me, she screams.

"You are in big trouble," she says as if this will stop me. Her long, skinny legs run away from me.

There is red paint on my face, chalk dust in my throat, and sharp pains in my hand. My knees are scraped and stained deep red, but I keep writing, crawling along the sidewalk until I am nose to nose with Mr. Martinez's brown suede shoes. He yanks me up by the collar of my shirt and wakes me from a dream.

I open my eyes on a vision. The words I have written along the narrow open corridor do not look like words at all. They are designs, laugh lines, braided threads of color. It is in code. I cannot remember how to translate them. I am ordered to clean the walls and sidewalk after school. Mrs. Oyama will supervise.

"They're so pretty. I hate to make you erase them," she says, staring with both hands on her hips, chewing on her bottom lip like she does in class when she's searching for the right words to describe a place on the map she has only seen in a book.

"They look like Arabic prayers," she says. Among the lines and circles, dots and dashes, I can make out prayers for my father never to leave me and for my mother to come back to us. Mrs. Oyama asks me if I know about Nommo, the African concept of the power of the word.

"You must learn to use your breath and your voice and old-fashioned paper to express your ideas." She puts her warm hand to my throat. As part of my punishment, I must write a letter of apology to the school. I will write the letter in my new language, though no one will understand.

Mrs. Oyama sits at a table in the schoolyard, grading papers and occasionally looking up to make sure I am scrubbing with the stiff brush I have been given. The strong soap and ammonia stings my eyes. Mrs. Oyama walks over to me and puts her hand on my shoulder.

"Are you sad?"

Her voice is like a pair of scissors stabbing me in the eye. I curl up on the sidewalk on a soft bed of words that can't be erased. I roll over onto my back and look up into the watery sky as if that will make her and the pain in the center of my body go away.

She kneels beside me, holding my hand. I am so close to telling her everything. The grandfather's face is on my tongue, but turns sour in my throat. It is too peaceful, too quiet, to open such a dangerous door. I tell her other things. She nods as if she understands the words tumbling out of my mouth like crooked letters. She sweeps her loose hair behind her ears and holds my hand. For this small tenderness I am forever grateful. I want to be with her all the time. Near her jasmine smell, touching her thick dark hair, looking into her smoky eyes. When she smiles her round face lights up and her eyes almost vanish. She is a small, compact woman with a collage of African and Asian features. She wears simple long-waisted dresses that drop nearly to her ankles. There is always lace covering her bosom. I imagine that there are lemons underneath the lace. Small, tight, juicy lemons.

"*W*here do you live?" Mrs. Oyama asks.

"In West Hollywood."

"Let me give you a ride home. I'd like to meet your father." She straightens her lace collar.

"He's not there." I pick at the scrapes on my knees.

"What time does he get home from work?" Her hand is on my shoulder.

I wonder if I can really trust her. When I remember how she held my hand and wiped my face with a cool cloth I decide that I want to.

"Wednesday."

Mrs. Oyama takes me home with her. We ride there in her little black Volkswagon that jerks along the street like a coughing turtle. Her house is in the Valley. A small white stucco house on a dead-end street. There is an avocado tree and a tangle of wild green fern in her front yard. She opens the door to her house and tells me to make myself at home. I don't really know what that means so I sit on her black leather sofa using my best posture. The smell of spicy food hangs in the air. She seems to notice it too. I can see her walking around in the kitchen beyond the breakfast bar. She opens windows and we are rewarded with a cool afternoon breeze. From my spot on the sofa I look around the large cluttered room. I imagined her house small and neat like her. The house is filled with objects that seem to breathe. Oriental fans and vases, African masks, carvings and cloths, hand puppets, porcelain dolls and woven rugs, platters of wooden fruit, bowls of dead flowers floating in cloudy water, and books, stacks of them everywhere, with papers stuck in them every which way.

"Your house looks like a museum," I say, fastening my eyes on one thing, then another. I pick up a beautiful blue bowl with a long thin crack running through its center.

"I collect things. My mother calls it junk. My father calls them collectibles. I call them memories. I found that broken bowl on a beach in Greece. The colors reminded me of a bowl my grandmother used to serve rice in when we would visit her." She opens the refrigerator and pours herself a glass of white wine.

"Would you like some juice?"

"Yes, please." She pours me orange juice into a clear long-stemmed glass just like hers.

We sit facing each other at opposite ends of the couch. She asks me questions about my life in Georgia and lets me talk without interruption for a long time. I tell her about my mother and my aunts and my best friend Joy. I tell her about my father and how lonely I feel in Los Angeles. She listens, sipping from her glass, murmuring and nodding. We let the walls talk. We play games using words with double meanings to deepen our conversation. We giggle like girls and eat the terrible dry eggs she scrambles for dinner with slices of avocado dipped in brown sugar for dessert. After drinking two glasses of wine, Mrs. Oyama begins to tells me things as if I am an adult. She confides in me. After three glasses she tells me to call her Iris, and I understand that this is our secret. After dinner she goes into her bedroom and comes out wearing a short flowered nightshirt and long loose white pajama bottoms. She pours us both cups of hot green tea.

"Where are you from?" I blurt out, not knowing how else to ask her where she got her Asian eyes, Indian nose, African mouth, half kinky hair, and strange cooking skills.

"I was born in San Francisco." She sits down on the floor next to the sofa and takes a sip of green tea pressing her hair behind her ears.

"I mean, what are you? Are you black?" I ask this because in Georgia it seemed you could be only one of two things, the other was white.

"My mother is black. She's a poet from North Carolina. My father's a Japanese journalist from a little town outside of Tokyo. They met at university and forty-five years later they're still together." She laughs, taking another sip of tea, steam clouding her half smile. "No one thought it would last a weekend."

"Don't you get scared here by yourself?" I ask her.

She is startled by my urgent question. She puts her teacup carefully beside her plate and begins to cut her avocado slices into small neat squares, chewing each morsel for a long time. She catches me watching her intently. "I don't want to be anyone's mother." She puts her fork down. She speaks as if she can read my mind.

In my mind we are mother and daughter. Man and wife. Bride and groom. Lover and beloved. I am a young boy and an old man. A baby girl and a pirate who has discovered the Rosetta Stone. In my father's clothes I can seduce her if I want, so smooth she won't even notice I'm pretending.

"I have a mother," I say. "I need somebody to be my friend."

She seems relieved. She starts talking quickly to cover her nervousness. Words pour out of her mouth so fast they seem blurry.

"I wasn't always alone. I married my best friend to save him from the immigration officers. He was my father's student. A very sweet man. From Osaka. We had never even held hands. After the wedding he suddenly wanted to exercise his marital rights. I'd never slept with a man and was shocked at his insensitivity. I got pregnant soon after we were married. I decided to try to make a life with him. One summer my husband went home to visit his sick grandmother. He took our three-year-old son with him. They never came back." She stretches her arms above her head and yawns. When she leans back into the sofa her nightshirt rides up and I can see the stretch marks on her belly. Long pale snakes ripple down her sides and mark her skin like whip marks.

"They disappeared," she says.

She seems to be embarrassed after she tells me this as if she didn't mean to and now she is silent and I want so badly to hear the sound of her voice. She jumps up from the floor, spilling her tea on the carpet.

"You can sleep on the sofa." Her voice is sharp. She loans me a tee shirt that belongs to her nephew, a football player at USC.

We make up the sofa with jasmine-scented sunflower sheets.

"Good night." She gives my arm an awkward pat. I reach out my arms to hug her. At first her body stiffens, but then she relaxes, gives my back a quick squeeze, then disentangles herself from my embrace. I miss this kind of touch. When the lights are out, I imagine I am at home and Mrs. Oyama and I both belong here. When I think she is asleep I walk down the hallway to her room. She has left her door open. I sit on the floor in the hall and watch her sleep, close my eyes and listen to the sound of her breathing. I lay down with the sharks and dream.

*My mother is dead, but I do not suffer sadness, I draw from the well of my memory the sweet taste of water, the deep swell of a soul kiss as it spreads through my body like hot honey. My mother's breasts feel like clouds in my tiny hands, her nipple is a comfort to my mouth and I cling to it.*

The next morning Mrs. Oyama finds me asleep across the threshold of her bedroom.

"Were you afraid?" she says, kneeling beside me.

"No. Were you?" I ask, remembering how she tossed and turned in her sleep. When I touch her by accident her skin is soft and damp. The nightshirt clings to her body.

"You're very pretty. You have the loveliest eyes," she says to me. I look away from her smoky eyes, embarassed and delighted. She talks almost nonstop about all the places she's traveled while she cooks a breakfast of peppery salmon croquettes with wasabi, lumpy yellow grits, and burnt toast.

"Did you look for them?" I ask. "Your husband and your baby." Her eyes darken.

"They disappeared. Mariah, don't wait for the wind to blow you a kiss," she says as if she knows something I don't. I bite down on her words. "Take control of your life." She becomes my geography teacher again and we are out of her house and on the freeway and I move my body from class to class though I don't remember how I've gotten from one place to another.

I open the door to the apartment on Wednesday after school and Matisse is lying on the unmade daybed asleep. He wakes with a start.

"Where have you been? I was out of my mind worrying about you when I got home last night." Matisse makes me take him to Mrs. Oyama's house. He doesn't believe I stayed with her. He doesn't speak to me the whole way there.

When Mrs. Oyama opens her door she looks first at me, then at my father. Her eyes make a cast of him. She begins to shine.

"I'm sorry to bother you but Mariah said she was with you while I was out of town. When I came back and she wasn't home, I almost called the police," he says.

"Come in, Mr. Santos. It's good to meet you. I'm glad you came. We should talk." Her voice is different. She sounds as if she is singing. Her small body is even smaller in his presence. My father makes me wait in the car while he sits on Mrs. Oyama's black leather sofa. I know that she is telling him everything she knows about me. I listen to songs on the radio and sing along with the ones I know. Matisse looks sad when he comes out.

"I wish I could make you happy," he says.

"I'm happy," I say, wishing it were true. He takes me to Griffith Park and we walk around with our arms around each other's waist, lost in our own thoughts like distant lovers.

*I am standing at Mrs. Oyama's door wearing my father's white suit. When she opens the door she looks as if she has seen a ghost. "You look like your father," she says, inviting me in for hot green tea.*

Mrs. Iris Oyama introduces me to the world of geography. She teaches me how to read maps. Maps of places I've never been are spread out for me like a meal. She marks out the four directions on the map of my heart and I remember that if you feel lost you follow the one you love and go where your love takes you.

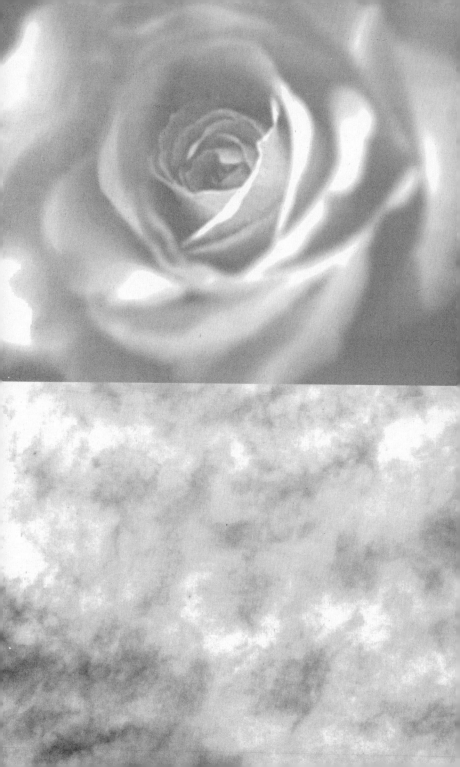

TWELVE

"When I was a little boy, I would run after every white fishtail Cadillac I saw. I thought my father was the only person who had one. His *was* the only one with wine-colored seats and yellow trim." Matisse maneuvers the Renault through the heavy freeway traffic, weaving between the cars. I like it when he talks about his father even though he doesn't. His face becomes an open window through which I can see the places he hurts.

"Poppy, we used to call him. It seemed like he was always traveling and I was always waiting for him. After dinner I would sit on the porch in the dark till mother made me come in and go to bed. He would promise to take my sister and me to baseball games and puppet shows in the park if we minded Mother and did well in school. Unlike my sister I was a straight A student, but as good as I was at home and at school, neither of us would get anything but ignored. When Poppy came home from the road I had things to tell him, drawings to show him, but he was too tired, too hung over, or too busy playing in local clubs to pay us much attention. Unless he was showing us off to his running buddies. It took a while but finally I decided to do what I wanted."

At last Matisse is taking me to his studio in an industrial park in South Central, the place he goes most nights. I don't know why he's been so reluctant to bring me here. Maybe the same reason he doesn't like to talk about his father. It is another sunny, blue sky day in L.A., and even the brightly colored rundown houses with dirt yards protected by decorative steel bars look pretty.

The old candy factory doesn't smell sweet at all, but is heavy with the aroma of stale coffee, turpentine, and drying paint. Stacks of canvases are leaned against a back wall. His studio, one of four in the building, is long and narrow with a high ceiling. Track lighting glides along one paint-splashed concrete wall. Windows have been roughly cut out along the top of the opposite wall. I can see the sky and a few clouds arranging themselves into swirls of pale blue cotton candy.

"Stand over there against the wall. In the corner." He picks up a large drawing pad and a small piece of charcoal.

"Do you want me to pose?" I put one hand on the hip of my blue jeans in what I think is a glamorous attitude.

"Be yourself." He sits on one end of a lumpy green sofa and begins to sketch me. I lean against the wall and look at the clouds floating against the sky while Matisse works quietly. After a while I take a peek over at him. His hand is no longer moving across the page; the charcoal he's holding is poised over the paper but it isn't moving. He is staring at me as if I have become a bird, wings and all.

"Have you ever kissed a boy?" he asks.

I turn away from his gaze, take several steps across the room. I flip through his canvases, seeing only flashes of color.

"I was just wondering if we need to have a talk. About . . . sex." He is so awkward I almost feel sorry for him, but I continue to avoid his eyes, push my hands deep into the pockets of my blue jeans and stroll around the room as if I am in Aunt Merleen's garden inspecting her tomato plants. Something is growing between us. He watches and waits. I let him suffer.

"You can tell me anything . . . ask me anything you want." He pauses. "I know you watch the movies in the closet . . ."

I don't want to hear another word. I gather my arms close to my body and walk out of the studio, my eyes mopping the dirty concrete floor, taking care to shut the door behind me. Four songs play on the car radio before he comes out. I don't want to look at him. I am smothered in a cloud of shame. We ride home in a thick silence that becomes familiar as we begin a journey into dangerous territory.

We didn't stay long that first time, but Matisse's studio has left an impression on me. Now I can see him. When he goes out at night, I can imagine him stripped to the waist applying ice-blue paint to a canvas with his fingers while my mother lies naked on the floor. I hope he never mentions the movies in the closet again, because if he does I will pour cement in my ears and seal my eyes shut with cold honey.

It's been a year since I've seen the seasons change. Every day the sky is perfect and blue or gray with pollution or wet with rain. One day in midsummer on a perfect blue day there is a knock at the door. I'm home alone. When I ask who is there, a woman's voice says, "It's Corinna. Joe El Jr.'s sister. Is he home?"

I've never heard anyone call my father that. I open the door. A woman is standing there in dark pumps, pale hose, a tailored navy blue suit. A lemon yellow scarf is elegantly knotted at her neck. Her hair is pulled back into a loose french braid. Her face is a perfect mask of makeup. It is as if my father has come home dressed like a woman.

"You must be Mariah," she says, stepping past me into the apartment. She stands in the middle of the room and takes a cigarette out of her purse and waits a few seconds as if someone will light it for her. She takes out a small gold lighter and a flame eats at the tip of her long, thin cigarette. She blows smoke from between her brick-colored lips and looks around the room. I follow her as she takes herself on a tour of the house.

"Your mother was a very pretty young woman," she says, straightening one of Matisse's paintings on the wall.

"She still is." I have found my tongue, but not the nerve to ask her what she is looking for.

"So you've heard from Coral?" She stops and turns around to face me just outside the bathroom in the narrow hallway.

"I mean she's not dead." I feel trapped in the small space.

"Our father wanted Joe El to marry her. That would have been the best thing to anchor him. Has he gotten a steady job yet, or is he still playing the part of the struggling artist?" She strolls into his bedroom and over to the window. She lifts the blinds and stares out at the busy street.

"He is an artist. A good one." I don't like her. She is cold and distant but tries to pretend that we are having a conversation. I sit down on the floor next to my father's bed and pick at stray threads in the carpet. I feel the need to protect him.

"Where do you sleep?" She catches me off guard.

I point toward the other room. A flicker of surprise, then disapproval crosses her face. She walks toward the living room. I get up and follow her.

"When is Joe El coming back?" She paces around, suddenly nervous.

I shrug my shoulders. I don't know what to do with my hands so I stand in the middle of the room staring at her back and start peeling my cuticles, biting off the excess.

"This evening?" I shrug my shoulders again. "Tomorrow?" I repeat the gesture, sucking on the edge of my thumb.

"Sometimes he sleeps in his studio." My fingers start to bleed.

"Don't do that, they'll get infected. How do you like L.A.?" She flicks the ashes from her cigarette into the ficus tree and turns to stare at me.

"It's okay." I wish I could tell her to leave.

"Maybe you could come up to Seattle and stay with us for a while. My girls are away at math camp, but they'll be home in a few weeks. What have you been doing all summer?"

At that moment Matisse enters the apartment. I am relieved, but when he sees his sister he backs up and looks as if he wants to run away.

"We've been worried about you," she says, reaching for him. They hug and seem to forget that I am in the room. He pulls away from her and leans his back against the front door.

"That's not why you're here." He looks at her blankly, waiting.

"Poppy's dead," she chokes on the words.

My father's expression doesn't change.

"When?" he asks. There is a soldier in his voice.

"Last night. We tried to call you." Her tears are ruining her makeup. My father reaches out to embrace her.

At Aunt Corinna's suggestion we go out to dinner and she talks and smokes the whole time. She talks about plans to take me back to

Seattle with her and plans to get Matisse a job in her firm. I can't get used to her calling him Joe El Jr.

"Uncle Jimmy called me. He said you borrowed a lot of money from him." She exhales a cloud of smoke that makes her face look ghostly.

"That was between him and me." My father sips his scotch and pretends to listen to what she is saying. I take my cue from him and eat the food in front of me, not speaking unless my aunt asks me a question which isn't often. I look around the restaurant and there are white people and black people and Asians and Mexicans all eating together and I realize this wouldn't be a calm evening in Georgia. Race-mixing would be cause for a riot.

"Why didn't you tell us what's been going on?" She stabs her food angrily.

"So Poppy could tell me what a bum I am? I'm doing fine. That was just a temporary thing. Uncle Jimmy had no right talking to you." My father sucks down the rest of his scotch like water.

"He was concerned, Joe El. It's not just about you anymore. You've got Mariah to think of." My father is silent. I keep my eyes on my half-eaten plate of spaghetti, wishing I could disappear. She talks about me as if I am not at the table. I stare at the blue lapis stone in her left earring and jazz plays softly in my ear until she stops talking. Matisse orders another scotch and drinks it down even faster than the first.

When the bill comes my father doesn't argue, he lets her pay with her gold American Express card. Outside it is night. Hollywood Boulevard is full of activity. Matisse helps Aunt Corinna on with her jacket.

"I'm sorry about Poppy, but I still don't have any reason to go back to Seattle."

Before Aunt Corinna can say anything, the valet drives up in her large rented silver Mercedes. Matisse takes my arm and we walk away from his sister. We leave her standing on the sidewalk open-mouthed with a burning cigarette in her hand.

A few blocks away Matisse opens the driver's side of his car and gets in. After a moment of fumbling with the keys in the ignition he slides over to the passenger seat and motions for me to come around to the other side.

"You drive," he says, his jaw set tight.

I get in and fasten my seat belt. I turn on the car and take a couple of deep breaths before easing carefully into traffic.

"Turn left at the light, you're gonna get on the freeway." His voice is hard.

My hands are shaking. I've never driven on a highway before. I grip the steering wheel and follow his directions. To keep up with the other cars I have to drive fast and pretty soon I'm feeling good. I like the feeling of being in control. I mostly keep my eyes on the road, but every now and then I look over at Matisse to see if he will tell me what to do next. He tells me when I can change lanes and which exit to take. I'm not really in control, I'm just driving. I drive and drive until we reach the desert. Matisse is asleep beside me, his left hand rests on my thigh. On a stretch of desolate highway the car and I seem to be one perfect thing flying just above the earth before taking off into the night sky.

"I'm sorry about your dad," I say. "Granddad." The word sounds foreign in my mouth.

We park at a truck stop on the edge of the desert. I wish I had words that would comfort him.

"I love you, Daddy."

"I love you more." He hugs me hard and close for a long time. He smells a little like jasmine. I feel safe in his arms. Completely.

My father cries softly, his head leaned against my shoulder, his left hand on my thigh. I put my arm around his shoulder and stroke his hair. Our breathing rises and falls together.

He could have sent me away or left me but he chose to stay and I choose him too. We are alone in the world and I want to give him everything. I want to absorb the sadness he feels for losing his father, cancel it out so that we can be a happy family. I would do anything for him.

"Let's go back." He directs me back to the city, and to the candy factory in South Central. He gets out of the car, opens my door for me, and we go inside his studio.

I am tired and sleepy. My shoulder aches from driving with his head leaned against me. He walks slow, his shoulders seem to sag. We sit at opposite ends of the lumpy green sofa. After a while he gets up and pours himself a glass of scotch. He goes to a corner of the studio, then comes back to sit beside me. He pulls opens a large sketch pad filled with drawings of my mother . . . naked . . . draped . . . sitting . . . standing . . . leaning . . . stretching . . . dancing . . . sleeping. He shows me a dozen small paintings of her in rich, earthy colors. She seems close enough to touch.

I know what he wants and I am willing. I take off my jacket and sit on the stool in front of him.

He sits on the sofa staring at me. The charcoal glides slowly across the page.

"Take off your shoes," he says, looking at my feet. I untie my sneakers and stuff my socks inside. He is drawing my naked feet yet it feels like he's holding them in his hands. My whole body is warm. He pauses. His weepy red eyes burn a hole through my clothes. He seems to be waiting. I unbutton my shirt and drop it on the floor. I unhook my bra, let it fall. Unzip my jeans and push them along with my panties down my legs over my ankles.

I take a pillow from the sofa and put it on the stool. I take my seat again, sit with both my hands in my lap, legs crossed at the ankle, back straight, eyes turned toward the morning sky.

I can hear his hands moving faster across a new page in his sketch book. I don't feel naked. I feel like I am already a painting, an object, like a bowl of fruit, something useful that eases his sadness. I feel close to him.

All summer long I am naked for my father.

$\mathcal{M}$atisse begins leaving me colorful little pictures on miniature canvases leaned against my pillow. On the back he writes lines from romantic poems in obscure languages. I comfort him every way I know how. I cook for him, take his clothes to the laundry, wait up for him like a worried wife. No matter what time he comes home he kisses me on the forehead. Sometimes he smells like Mrs. Oyama. I don't ask why. I like it that they are friends too.

$\mathcal{I}$n Matisse's studio my nude body is floating in blue water, dancing in blue light, skipping rope under a blue moon. He is fascinated by my body and the color blue. Even though the faces are turned away from the eye, the naked bodies on the wall in his studio are mine. I am not only naked but my innermost thoughts seem visible underneath the surface of my skin. Now he asks me to model naked for him in the most vulnerable positions. For hours sometimes he makes me lean with my back against the wall in his studio facing him, breasts forward, arms covering my face. Sometimes I am crying from the pain of standing still for so long, but he doesn't seem to notice. We rarely speak during these sessions when he is looking at me and I am looking up at the sky or at slices of the moon. Afterward, he buys me something pretty. Once he bought me a heart-shaped ring. Another time a blue velvet hat, an antique perfume bottle, a dozen yellow roses. The only thing I want is for him to be my father. He says he wants to be my friend.

At school I have made a new friend since Candy and Bertine were expelled. My new friend Song is a tough Korean girl whose adopted parents are older white hippies who take her to antinuclear rallies and peace marches on the weekend. Her short hair is black and shiny, her round face is always set hard until she sees me. Then she smiles and punches me gently on my shoulder. We smoke in the bathroom before school and cut classes to go shopping at the mall. We talk about how we will change the world when we are adults and in charge, but for now Song is concerned about our social lives.

"Are you going to the graduation dance?" she asks as we stroll the mall.

"Nobody asked me."

"Nobody asked me either, but I'm going anyway. We could dress up like cowgirls or something."

"Give me a better reason."

"We could get my brother to take us to a nightclub after the dance and get drunk to celebrate the fucked-up world we're graduating into. Come on, it could be fun. My brother's friend David is coming down from San Francisco State for the weekend. The four of us could go together, make a night of it. What do you say?"

Song is so convincing.

*T*he colors he uses are rich, the bodies he paints are fleshy and voluptuous, playful. He asks me to pose for him whenever he is inspired, which could be any time of the day or night, for a few minutes or a few hours. His paintings are inspired by his namesake, the murals of Diego Rivera, and the collages of Romare Bearden. I get lost in his wild rivers of color.

I am determined to break the long dark silences between us.

"What do you remember most about my mother?" I ask, as he concentrates on my breasts with his eyes.

"I remember everything," he says. "Don't move." His brush teases the canvas in front of him.

"Tell me."

"Tell you?" he repeats, distracted, and takes a drink from his glass of scotch.

"All the details. You said we shouldn't keep any secrets. Tell me everything you know." I am willing to beg for just one memory.

He flirts with me as if I were someone he barely knows. I blush. I am sitting on a sofa, looking out of the big windows at the cloudless sky, bare-breasted, with a piece of African kente cloth wrapped around my waist.

"Will you tell me your secrets, *señorita*, if I tell you mine?" He winks at me.

I almost tell him about what happened in Texas, but I am afraid he will be mad at me.

"She told me about you," I say, scratching an itch discreetly.

"What did she say about me?" Suddenly he is alert.

"That it was winter-spring-summer and fall when you met. She said that there was a hurricane-blizzard-earthquake on the moon where you met. She told me a lot of stories about you. I didn't know what to believe."

"Your mother liked to tell stories. She had a . . ."—he searches for a word—". . . vivid imagination."

"She's not dead."

"I didn't say . . ."

"She said you were a good painter."

"That's how I tell my stories. I only knew your mother for a few weeks, but she is here. She will always be here," he says, pointing to his chest. He takes a deep breath and smiles a sad smile.

This is the story Matisse tells me about my mother:

"The first time I saw Coral she was wearing white from head to toe. I thought she was an angel until I realized that I was in a hospital. I licked my lips when I saw her. She had the most gentle hands and a charming southern accent that made her sound like she was singing instead of talking. I forgot about falling off that ladder. I forgot about the pain in my head. When we were alone in the examining room, before I could think of anything to say, I kissed her on the lips. She pulled away and petted me like a new puppy. She cleaned the cut on my head and put a bandage on it. She told me to go home, get some rest, but I waited six hours until her shift was over and offered to drive her home. We spent the next couple of weeks locked up in my apartment loving each other. And then she was gone and I thought I'd dreamed her up."

"Why did she leave?" I ask.

"She had to report to the military hospital in Kansas."

"Didn't you try to see each other again?"

"She fell in love with somebody else and I never saw her again. She wrote to tell me that she had left you with her aunts down in Georgia because she was sick. I haven't heard from her since then." He takes my hand in his and strokes it.

"I felt like nobody really wanted me."

"I'm going to love you now." He kisses my cheeks. Fresh tears wet my face.

"Cry," he says, "Daddy's here." He takes me in his arms. His warm hands rub slow circles into the small of my back.

*I* don't tell Matisse that what I really want is to dance with Mrs. Oyama in a white linen suit, to kiss Song on the lips, to sleep all night in the safety of his arms.

Song says her brother has agreed take me to the dance. Matisse is not impressed that Song's brother is a freshman at UCLA.

"You're too young to go out with boys," he says.

"I'm almost seventeen. Anyway, it's not like he's my boyfriend."

"No," he says and refuses to discuss it anymore.

A week before the graduation dance, Matisse feels guilty about not letting me go. He decides to take me out on a special date. Dinner and dancing. Mrs. Oyama helps me pick out a long black jersey dress with a scoop neck, sling-back low-heeled silver sandals, and a heart-shaped silver necklace to match my heart-shaped ring. Matisse is dressed in a rented tux and wears the silver cuff links I have bought him with the money my aunts gave me. I am going out on my first date with my father and I am nervous. Before we leave the apartment Matisse kisses me on my cheek.

"You look beautiful," he says. "You look so much like your mother."

I blush and straighten his tie. He pulls the car out of the garage and waits out front for me. I float down the stairs. Happiness is not a word, but the world I live in as we sail through the streets in our carriage. I am wrapped in tiny silver blinking lights. We laugh and sing along with the radio. At the downtown hotel where we are having dinner, the valet parks our car as Matisse takes my arm and leads me along the red carpet under the elegant white canopy into the hotel lobby glittering with chandeliers and cluttered with groups of jeweled women in shiny dresses, drenched in perfume, their features clouded with heavy makeup. Their glassy-eyed men look bored and uncomfortable in their suits and tuxedos. I feel as though everyone is staring at us because my father is so handsome and I feel so beautiful. I am the happiest girl in silver sandals when we enter the ballroom. I am surprised to see Mrs. Oyama standing by the bar in a strapless sparkling white sequined dress.

My father drags me across the room to the bar. He lets go of my arm to give Mrs. Oyama's hand a kiss.

"Mariah, you look so grown up. You're a beautiful young lady," she says and smiles a big smile. Then she looks into my father's grinning eyes.

"How about drinks for the two most beautiful women in the room?" Matisse asks, his eyes on Mrs. Oyama's tiny breasts.

"How about a Pink Lady, Mariah?" she asks, giving me with a little wink.

"I'll have a scotch and soda," I say. Mrs. Oyama looks like a movie star. I lean back against the bar drinking her up with my eyes. Flowers bloom in the air around her. Jasmine.

"Not tonight, honey. How about a club soda?" my father says absently, then asks Mrs. Oyama to dance. He puts his arm around her shoulders and she smiles up at him.

"I want a scotch and soda." I insist, glaring at them. Jealousy is a snake that bites me.

"It's not going to happen, Mariah." I can tell he is losing his patience with me.

"Then I don't want anything." I turn away from them to flirt with the bartender wiping down the bar behind us. I wink at the old man and wave him over to me. When he reaches me I whisper to him loud enough for Matisse to hear.

"I'll have a scotch and soda."

"Mariah, what's wrong with you?" My father yells at me for the first time. I start to walk away from them across the dance floor when he grabs my arm and turns me around.

"What is your problem, young lady?" he whispers roughly. I shake off his grip and run away from him. He makes it inside the elevator at the same time I do. We get off on the twenty-third floor and he follows me in the maze of hallways. I huddle in the doorway of a linen closet crying.

"What's wrong, baby?" He kneels next to me. "Are you upset about Iris? I asked her to meet us here because I thought you liked her."

"I wanted to dance with you first."

He holds my hand and doesn't let it go of it for a long time. We take the elevator down to the ballroom. Mrs. Oyama is sitting at the bar. She looks worried. Matisse leaves me for a moment by the ladies' room. He whispers something to Mrs. Oyama, then gives her money for taxi fare home. He walks her to the door. She turns and waves good-bye to me. I wave back. There are no hard feelings. When Matisse comes back inside we act like new lovers on a holiday. After an elegant dinner in the hotel restaurant, we go to a nightclub on Hollywood Boulevard, dance to disco, salsa, and slow ballads as if there is no one in the world but us. No one else matters.

Later that night when he thinks I'm asleep, he leaves me alone again. I watch him drive away before setting up the film projector. After touching myself, I take three Valiums and fall asleep in his bed.

*At the moment my body engages in the promise of an orgasm I unfold a drawer full of sorrows and each one becomes a tear that melts down my face. I unfold Mama first. Pretty blue words. Tiger-print scarf. Pink satin slip. Scent of bergamot and click of high heels dancing on a hardwood floor. Then Aunt Merleen and Aunt Faith come undone. The last sorrow I unfold is Matisse. A wave of pain and pleasure washes over me.*

When I wake up Matisse is lying in bed with me underneath the covers. I wonder how long he has been there. I wonder if I am dreaming.

"Were you scared here by yourself?" he whispers hoarsely.

"No, I was sleeping. I didn't think you were coming back tonight." I turn my back to him. Flowers bloom in the darkness.

I can feel his erection on the back of my thigh. I roll away from the heat of his body. I am afraid of his whispery voice. I close my eyes and I see the grandfather's face. I feel my father's eyes on me and I panic. He reaches across the white space that separates us and begins stroking my hair, my shoulders, the back of Mama's pink slip.

Instinctively I curl my body into a ball. The man, my father, moves closer. My body becomes rigid and cold as his arm wraps around my waist. I search my voice for a word to stop him.

"Daddy?" I whisper. "Please don't hurt me." His arm slips away.

"I'm sorry, baby. I didn't mean anything. Don't be afraid of me. I'm not gonna hurt you. I'm sorry. I love you," he says desperately.

I wake myself up screaming. My father is nowhere to be seen. I am in bed alone. I am sweating, shaking with fear.

I never fall asleep in his bed again no matter how scared I am. I begin to avoid my father's eyes again. I am embarrassed by my thoughts about him, I wonder if he is aware of his. Dreams, my mama taught me, do not lie.

Some mornings I find empty scotch bottles beside his bed. We fight about my using his razor to shave my legs and underarms. We fight about dishes left in the sink overnight. We are not really fighting about those things, but something deeper has surfaced. He is sad because he has lost his father and he is scared because sometimes he forgets that I am his daughter.

"Daddy, are you okay?" I ask.

"Everything is fine," he says, but I don't believe him.

There is new growth in the ficus tree I have watered and tended. Words are beginning to sprout from the earth. I can't read them yet but they are there. Even though I try to keep my distance from him, I am close enough to know that my father is in pain. He wears his sadness like old clothes. Sometimes he comes home in the middle of the night, sits on the floor beside my bed, and watches me sleep.

I begin collecting words. Their meanings don't matter. I want to taste deliciously long vowels and sweet consonants, hear the sound of their music and eat the rich letters of memory like cake. *Pellucid* . . .

*winsome . . . vicissitudes . . . languish . . .* I collect foreign words. *Amore . . .
bisous . . . habibi . . . querencia . . .* Words with color, pitch, tone, texture,
shape, tang. I put them in my dream book and hide them under my
mattress. I boil them, bake them, fry them in hot grease and I feed on
them, trying to understand the life I am living with my father and without my mother. I want to go home to Aunt Faith and Aunt Merleen.
It's where I belong but I don't want to abandon Matisse.

Mrs. Oyama is the one who encourages me to to stay in school. I
wish she was my mother because then I would be home when she hugs
me close and kisses my hair. She invites me to her house some weekends when my father is away. I like being alone with her. I wonder if
she keeps my father company at night.

"Do you love my father?"

Mrs. Oyama stops washing the dishes and comes to sit next to me
at the breakfast bar.

"Mariah, your father is a good man but love isn't enough for him.
He needs more than either one of us can give him."

"I don't know what to do."

"Save yourself." She opens her mouth to speak, then decides on
another direction. "Do you have dreams, goals for your life?" She
arranges lemons in a red enamel bowl on the low table in front of us.

"I want to find words to tell the stories I wish I knew."

"Invent them, write happy endings, give hope where there is none."
She is convinced I can do this, but I am sure of nothing. When I leave
I won't say good-bye to her. I will slip away into the night and think
of her just like my mother thinks of me wherever she is. I will pray
for my father, invent rituals to heal him. But I have to save myself first.

Aunt Faith calls. Her voice is faint as if she is speaking from under
water.

"Your Aunt Merleen passed away last night." The stitches in my broken heart come undone with these words.

Now I have someone dead to cry for. My body feels a strange relief, but I cannot be comforted. Matisse is helpless. His grief is soothed by the time he gets to the bottom of a scotch bottle. Aunt Merleen is dead of a brain hemorrhage. I punch a hole in the wall of the apartment. I break the little finger of my left hand. It is not enough pain to distract me from the loss. Why did so much time pass?

"I'm sorry. I know she meant a lot to you," he says from across the room.

"Can I be alone for a while?"

"Sure, baby. I know what you're feeling."

"I just want to sleep."

He brings me a Valium and a short glass of water. I fall asleep on the floor next to the ficus tree that seems to be withering and dying before my eyes.

The next day Matisse says he doesn't want me to go back to Georgia, he is afraid he'll lose me, but I am afraid of what will happen if I stay. We yell at each other and he leaves me alone again. I lie on the daybed with the tv on for company. I want to drift into pleasant dreams, but I can't seem to relax. I take two more Valium and start watching an old movie. At some point I hear a soothing voice asking me questions.

"Do you need someone to talk to? Are you lonely? Sad? Do you need help?" Her voice is familiar.

"Yes," I answer, my eyes shut tight.

"Call me," the voice inside the television says, and I dial the numbers.

When a man answers, I ask to speak to the voice on the tv. He asks if he can help me and I say, "Nobody can help me but her." She sounds just like my mother.

"Hello. This is Ava, what's your name?" a woman says softly.

"Are you my mother?" I ask.

"No, I'm not your mother. What's your name?" She sounds so far away.

"Can you help me?"

"Have you been drinking or taking drugs?"

"I just wanted to sleep."

"What did you take?"

"She's dead."

"Somebody died on you, huh? I'm sorry about that. Where are you?"

"She taught me how to drive." I remember where she kept her softness.

"I want to help you, but you have to tell me where you are."

Suddenly I realize that my mother is not on the line. I hang up and fall into a deep, heavy dreamless sleep. When I wake up the next morning it is misty outside. A dull gray light filters through the curtains. I am lying in the middle of the floor when Matisse walks into the apartment. He looks to me just as my mother must have seen him in her dreams, his face and arms spattered with blue paint. He stinks of scotch and sweat. He hasn't bathed in days.

"I want to go home." I send the words up to him like arrows. They find their target.

"Are you sure?"

"Yes."

"Let's call your Aunt Faith to tell her you're coming," he says sadly. He sits on the floor next to the dead ficus tree.

"Baby, I'm sorry if I let you down. I want to be a good father to you. Write to me, okay? And if you need anything you call me. I'm here for you." I feel sorry for him, he is breaking my heart.

When I'm alone I give myself a tattoo using a needle and black thread. Suddenly I have power over the pain. I fish beneath the surface of my skin marking a code that can't be broken. Each time I pierce my skin it is as if a little more pain escapes and soon I will be empty and feel nothing. This is what I hope. I lift my skirt and stroke the tiny, bloody black lines written on my upper thigh. I stroke them to remind myself that I don't need to feel anybody else's pain, I have enough of my own. I play a lonely stretch of highway on the cello and Rosemary weeps bloody tears right along with me.

"Why did you send for me?" I ask.

"Because I wanted to get to know you. Because I thought it was the right thing to do. I thought it would work out."

At the bus station I hug my father awkwardly. He watches the bus until it disappears.

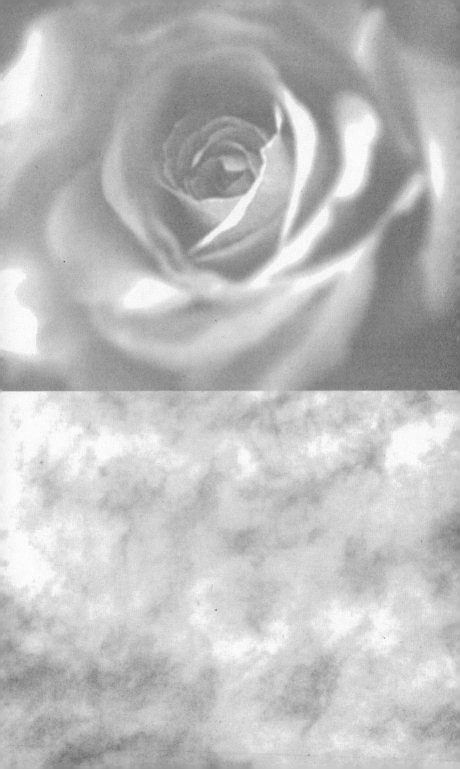

THIRTEEN

$\mathcal{I}$t is raining hard when the bus arrives at the station, rain so heavy it pulls tears down from my eyes. I can't see clearly through the windows, but I recognize the dark green fabric of Aunt Faith's raincoat dancing around her legs in the breeze. She is standing under the metal canopy next to the big blue car, shielding her eyes from the rain. She has gained weight. Her tiny green velvet hat is tilted to one side as if she has bumped into something. Her face is a bowl of pain. She is wearing a pale green house dress painted with leaves. She is a wide woman. She is soft as cake. We hug and kiss. Everything is wet.

"We missed you," Aunt Faith says, wedging her bulk behind the steering wheel and turning the key in the ignition. I can't believe Aunt Faith is driving. She used to be so afraid. Now she is more than seventy and what seemed impossible is happening right before my eyes. Suddenly I feel what must be pride filling my chest. I hope I will be as brave when I am an old woman on my own.

"I missed you more," I say, touching her shoulder. The car lurches forward into the street. "I can't believe you're driving."

"I told you I wouldn't be the second driver all my life, but I can't talk and drive," she says quickly as she hunches over the huge steering wheel trying to concentrate on staying in her lane.

"We've got plenty of time to talk," I say. I want to tell her how scared I was the first time Matisse let me drive his car on the freeway. I want to tell her so many things, but we have plenty of time. I am beginning to feel the swelling of roots under my feet. An ease settles over me as I shed miles of uncertain road.

Aunt Faith drives slowly along Fourth Avenue as traffic splashes past us. Car horns honk and swerve around us as she creeps along with her foot on the brake. She looks nervous. After another block she is sweating heavily. Finally she pulls the car over to the side of the road and turns off the engine. She is breathing so hard and fast I am afraid that she is going to lose conciousness.

"Baby, do you drive?" she asks, looking at the sheets of rain dashing against the winshield.

"Aunt Merleen taught me."

"Then you take us home. My eyes not what they used to be." We awkwardly switch places. I am the grown-up and she is the scared lit-

tle girl. I haven't driven in a long time, but I remember the most important things. I can hear Aunt Merleen's rough voice running down
the list as I comply.

*Pump the accelerator once with your right foot. Check mirrors. Key in the igni-
tion. Foot on brake. Emergency brake down. Headlights on. Shift car into drive. Left
blinker on. Check mirrors again. Look quick over your left shoulder. Keep both hands
on the wheel. Foot on the gas. Eyes on the road. Stay between the lines. Red light stop.
Green light go. Yellow light speed up. You can make it.*

I have no problem navigating the familiar streets to the big white
house across the tracks. The car drives smoothly over the bumpy road.
We are caught at the railroad crossing and must wait for a cargo train
to pass. Passenger trains don't come here anymore. I used to think
about taking the train to my mama, but I can't imagine it anymore.
She will have to come to me to explain all the miles and all the minutes I have had to spend without her. I saved a thousand good-nights
for her. Manhattan, Kansas, seems like a made-up place.

Suddenly the rain stops and the sun cuts through heavy clouds. I
roll down the window and swallow a chestful of clean, damp air.

"There's been some changes since you been gone," Aunt Faith says,
folding and refolding a lacy white handkerchief in her lap. I drive across
the tracks after the train passes. When we are a few blocks from the
house I see what she means. A small, white brick building has risen from
the lot where Masterson's used to be. Heavy black metal bars cross the
windows of a laundromat and a music store. Wooden benches out front
are decorated with young girls sitting on newspapers, pushing baby car-
riages, or dancing with boys to loud music blaring from speakers on
the front of the building. I can almost see myself standing there pushing a baby with eyes like honey. A muffled moan brings me back behind the steering wheel of the big, blue car. Aunt Faith is crying.

"You okay?" I ask, knowing that she is not.

"Something in my eye." She dabs at her eyes. The route home is
littered with memories.

Everything else is just as I remember it. The red brick school building, the public library, the liquor store, the row of shotgun houses, the housing projects, and the big white house that is home. I ease into the driveway and put the car in park, raise the emergency brake, and turn off the engine. Aunt Faith wipes sweat from underneath her chin with her chubby fingers. She struggles against the weight of gravity to raise herself out of the car. I help her up the back steps and into the house. Once inside, familiar smells wrap around me and draw me in. I expect to hear Aunt Merleen's thunderous footsteps on the back stairs or the sound of a blues tune humming in her throat. Instead the house is silent.

Aunt Faith begins to fade into the floral wallpaper. She is like an enormous spirit let loose without a purpose. Her love is gone, drained from her body like blood. Losing Merleen is like losing one of our senses. We want her back. We try to comfort each other, but this kind of grief is not easy to soothe. Me and Faith find a new routine, stepping around the holes in the air left by Aunt Merleen.

"The garden needs weeding," Aunt Faith says, looking out of the kitchen window.

"I'll do it in the morning after I take you to your doctor's appointment." I peel potatoes for our dinner. There is a numbness in my limbs that grows more pronounced each day. I aim to empty my mind.

I take care of Aunt Faith, whose diabetes, the doctor says, is getting worse. She drinks several cans of Coke a day and complains about having to pee every five minutes. Her skin is dry; even though I help her lather cocoa butter on every morning after her bath she scratches her arms all the time. I can see the shades coming down over her eyes. The doctor says Aunt Faith needs to have an operation to remove the cataracts clouding her eyes, but she refuses. Her memories of hospitals are filled with pain, loss, and suffering, so I don't press her. In her mind, she can still see the important things in focus. Her language is littered with visual images. Sometimes she fools me and I believe she can see the blue in my shirt, the smudge on a glass of water.

She thinks I need to keep my mind busy and suggests I enroll in summer school. I do it because I only need three classes to graduate and it means I won't have to sit through another year of high school. I sign up for math, English, and typing.

"Have you thought about where you want to go to college?" Aunt Faith asks in the car on the way to our Monday morning trip to the grocery store.

"No." I have not thought about what to do with my life beyond the mundane catalogue of hot humid summer days that pass quietly between the two of us.

"What about Clark or Spelman so you can stay close to home? We saved a little money, you know. Merleen thought you'd be a good teacher. Or maybe you could be a nurse like your mother." Aunt Faith puts her hand on my shoulder and squeezes it a little.

College seems so far away and foreign to me. Aunt Faith is so needy. If I went to college I would study languages. Perhaps like my mother I'll develop a taste for travel. I could peel back the surface of words and look around inside of them for deeper meaning. Maybe I'll feed on what I find and become someone no one would recognize.

"I'll think about it," I say and park the car across the street from the A&P underneath a flowering magnolia tree.

Sunday mornings we go to church. The mothers of the church are still falling out in the aisles and praying to God for salvation and for-giveness of present and future sins. I don't realize how much I have missed the singing until I become aware of my feet tapping out the old African rhythms in the songs.

"No finger popping in here," Aunt Faith whispers, swatting me on my thigh with her lavender-scented lace fan. I smile and snap my fin-gers in my mind. The music makes me feel happy. I feel as if I am filled with the spirit like the old ladies who shout from the amen cor-

ner, but I don't want everybody to know it so I shake my leg to the
beat of the music and try to find a way to pray that makes sense to
me. I pray for my father and I pray for Aunt Faith's health. I don't
want to be alone in the world.

Me and Aunt Faith go to the nursing home Sunday afternoons to
visit Grandma Gert, who sometimes refuses to speak to us. Aunt
Faith isn't afraid of her sister's sharp tongue anymore, she is simply
keeping a promise she made to visit her every week. I have made no
such promise to tolerate the killing stares and verbal abuse. I don't exist
for my grandmother and that is fine with me. When I have delivered
Aunt Faith to one of the nurses at the desk, I go back to the car and
listen to soul music on the radio until Aunt Faith is ready to go home.
Music is a train for me and I ride, hanging on to the rhythms as if
their grace will carry me along.

One Sunday I am sitting in the big blue car listening to James Brown
holler on the radio when I see a tall, skinny boy wearing a blue baseball cap, a red-and-cream-colored varsity jacket, and jeans. He is pushing a wheelchair filled with books tied down to the seat. He is pushing
toward me in the parking lot. His walk is a funky bounce, a rocking
from side to side as if he can hear the music on the car radio through
the rolled-up windows. As he gets closer I can see him smiling. I check
to make sure the doors are locked and feel for the hammer Aunt Merleen always kept under the seat in case of emergencies.

"You look like I'm gonna bite you," he says. I nearly fall over when
I realize that it is Deadman's half sister, Tree. I roll down the window.

"I thought you were a boy," I say before I can stop myself.

She laughs from deep in her throat.

"Sometimes I wish I was." She pulls off the baseball cap. "It's still
me, though."

Her hair is cut so close to her head I can almost see what she is
thinking. Up close she still looks like a boy. I blush and look away.

"What you doing out here by yourself?" she says, leaning into the car as if to smell my scent.

"Waiting for my aunt. She's visiting my grandmother." I take a deep breath. She smells fresh and clean like she's just taken a shower and sprinkled herself with baby powder.

"Who's your grandmother?" Her eyes search inside the car.

"Gertrude Rains." The name is like a rock in my mouth.

"Gert Rains is your grandmother? I don't mean any disrespect, but that is the meanest woman I ever met in my life. She bit a nurse on the hip last week and called her a frog-faced bitch. They had to tie her down." Tree shakes with laughter, but her smile fades when she sees the hardness in my eyes.

"I guess I'm lucky, she won't talk to me at all." I grip the steering wheel with both hands.

"She seems real sad. Always asking when her daughter is coming to see her. Is that your moms?"

"Yeah." There is an awkward silence.

"You seen Joy?" I tap my fingers on the steering wheel and shake my head. "We live together."

"You and Joy?" I say and she smiles at my surprise.

"Yeah. She got a baby by my brother, you remember Deadman. He's in jail again. Her sister Nicky got married and Joy had to move out of the trailer. She moved in with me a few months ago. You ought to come by and see us. Apartment 419 D in the row facing the playground. Joy talks about you all the time." Tree smiles at me. Her lips are so close I could kiss her. I wonder if the baseball park is open and if she would go with me to see a game next Sunday.

"You're the Hollywood girl. You're famous in our house. Joy keeps the card you sent her taped to the refrigerator," she says. "Let me give you our number."

The only postcard I mailed from L.A. was to Joy. It was a big flashy card with a picture of Sunset Boulevard on it. I ramble through the glove compartment looking for a pen.

After she has written down the number I stare at her long smooth fingers draped over the car door.

"Call anytime. And if you ever want your hair cut, I work at Deacon Long's barber shop, next to the Cut and Curl." I don't say anything because I am thinking about her fingers in my hair.

"I better get going, the ladies are waiting for me." She starts to move away from the car.

"You come every Sunday?" I want to hold her in my sight for just a few moments longer.

"Naw, my cousin works out here. She asked me to read to some of the old ladies on her wing." Now she seems shy and begins pushing the wheelchair toward the building behind us.

"Maybe I'll see you around. Tell Joy I'll call her." I wave at her, then feel silly about it and cover my mouth in embarassment. She winks at me.

"Later," she says, then pushes off. She looks back over her shoulder and smiles. I watch the back of her red jacket until it disappears inside the building.

Sunday evenings, just before sunset, me and Aunt Faith visit Aunt Merleen in Pine View Cemetery. I drive slowly, taking care to brake when the traffic light at Boulevard and Bridge Street turns yellow.

"Girl, you could've made that light," Aunt Faith says in her role as second driver. I smile and continue at my own pace toward the cool, green grassy field of dead relatives. Aunt Merleen is a sweet memory, but she is in the mouth of Aunt Faith as sure as there are seven days in a week. I carry two folding chairs in my left hand and offer my right elbow to Aunt Faith, guiding her over the hill of grass and under the tall oak tree.

Sometimes she forgets that I am there and they have conversations that explain all the years that held them together like the pages of a book. Aunt Faith sits in the folding chair, her hands clasped together as if in prayer. She closes her eyes and seems to travel far away from present time. Sometimes she drifts into a kind of sleep. Sometimes she speaks as if Aunt Merleen is standing in the square of earth before us.

"You right sister. Got nobody to call but each other, so let's don't argue no more. Let's just get the tomatoes planted before the next wet spell. You know them tomato plants grow twined together so tight nothing could separate them. Just like us." Aunt Faith clasps her fingers together tightly. "We didn't have to hide, nor hurry up our love. It seem to swell and grow every season. When you cultivate sweetness, then sweetness is bound to flourish. You are so good to me. What I would've done without you? Where I would've gone? You a blessing. You a true enough blessing." Aunt Faith limps slowly around the tree, her arms crossed at her waist like she is carrying her weight in her arms. She walks as if Aunt Merleen walks beside her. I sit and watch, listen and wait for Aunt Faith to let me know when it is time to leave.

That they were so close seems to me as natural as the grass covering Aunt Merleen's grave and as right as the color blue for the sky above us. Seeing their life from the inside makes me believe that it is possible to live in the rich shelter of longtime love.

"Let's go home," Aunt Faith says. "I'm tired."

I take her arm and we make our way back to the big blue car.

Aunt Faith begins to take on gestures that were once Merleen's. Her laughter becomes loud, she sings the blues and sits in the garden in back of the big white house listening to Merleen's flowers grow.

Faith is losing her sight, but she gains strength in her other senses. Her thickly veined hands, each finger graced with a gold or silver band, each wrist a song of silver bangles, tests the air for obstacles with a snake-handled ebony cane. She shows me how to see without my eyes.

She teaches me to test the ground I stand on, to see obscured memories and to navigate through my river of pain. Aunt Faith can't see, but she can feel just fine, and she is teaching me how.

*M*y fingers are shaking when I dial Tree's number. Joy answers and screams my name when she hears my voice.

"Tree say she saw you a month ago at the nursing home. Where you been?"

"I'm in summer school."

"Why?"

"Aunt Faith wants me to start college next year."

"You aren't going away, are you? You just got back."

"I don't know yet."

"Now don't you get dusty up in that big, old house. Come see us. Tree's been wondering when you was gonna come." I decide right then that I will go to see Joy.

Aunt Faith doesn't respond right away when I tell her I'm going to the projects to visit Joy.

"Did you hear me, Aunt Faith? I'm going across the street to see Joy."

She looks in my direction from her seat by the back door and nods her head in acknowledgment that she has heard me. The short walk across the street and half a block down the broken sidewalk is like entering another world—loud colors flap on clotheslines in back yards, loud voices gather on porches, and loud music blares from open windows. Joy and Tree are sitting on the front porch. Joy is on the phone but she stands up in her short cut-off jeans and halter top and waves me over.

"Do you want something to drink?" Tree asks. She is wearing a blue mechanic's uniform that is too big for her. I am surprised to see pink frosted nail polish on her toes. She sees me looking and points toward Joy, who is making faces and motioning that she is trying to end the conversation.

"No. I just came by to say hi." I sit down on the bottom step and stare at Tree's pink toes. Joy hangs up the phone with a loud sigh and hugs me from behind. She acts as if I died and came back to life before her eyes. It is as if no time has passed; she is still my friend.

When she is not yelling at her oldest child not to eat the dirt he is playing in, Joy talks about men, how she misses Deadman when she goes to bed at night. Deadman, she tells me, went back to jail for trying to organize the workers into a union at the A&P down the street. She listens for the sound of Deadman's baby in a crib behind the screen door.

I visit Joy and Tree every few days. We drink beer and remember the old times. It becomes our habit to sit on Joy's porch in the evening watching her children play, listening to the soul music station on the radio, and combing each other's hair. Tree doesn't say much and neither do I. I can't read her. Sometimes she is so quiet, like she's taking notes or something. She goes to bed early and gets up late to go to the barber shop to cut heads. Joy watches her children and her soaps and cooks dinner for Tree and the babies. We watch young men in tight jeans, baggy work clothes, and suits strut past us and we comment on their hair, their eyes, their physique. We watch young women with the same keen eye and suddenly the world seems so full of possibilities for love and sex and happiness in each pair of work boots and pumps that walks by.

Joy says waiting for Deadman isn't so bad, at least she knows he is coming home someday. She had his baby boy.

"A son is worth something," she says, rocking the child to sleep in her arms.

One day Joy asks about my mother, breaking the unspoken rule not to discuss her. I become a turtle seeking shelter behind a hard shell of old wounds.

"I don't want to talk about her," I say a little too quickly.

"I was just wondering if you've heard from her," Joy says.

"It's been a long time, huh?" Tree says.

"She'll be back when she can. I don't want to talk about her." I say this too loudly and it comes out harsh but I don't apologize. I just walk away from them, down the block and across the street to the safety of the big white house.

"I could eat a whole red velvet cake by myself," Aunt Faith says, rubbing her large arthritic hands across her grumbling belly as she shuffles into the kitchen wearing Aunt Merleen's old leather mules. It seems as if she says these things just to irritate me.

"You're not supposed to eat sugar."

"That young doctor said I could have most anything in moderation." She is testing my patience.

I ignore her. If I say anything she'll say I'm talking back, and after all, according to her, she is still the only grown woman in the house. I am at the kitchen table trying to read the directions on her insulin bottle. A nurse will start coming to teach me how to give Aunt Faith the shots. She says that I can practice on oranges. The needles are sharp and my hands shake remembering how my mama used to give me shots when I was sick with a cold. I'd cry, but she'd make me lie down on my stomach and close my eyes.

"Think of a pretty word," Mama would say just before the needle pierced the flesh of my behind. I'm afraid that I'll hurt Aunt Faith or end up giving myself a shot. She never complains about the pain. I am becoming used to caring for her. I don't have time to think about my own life.

"That was your mama's favorite kind of cake," she continues as if I haven't spoken. She hands me the ragged-edged recipe card.

## Red Velvet Cake

1-1/2 cups cooking oil or 1
   stick of unsalted butter
1 teaspoon vinegar
3 eggs
1 bottle of red food coloring
1 teaspoon of vanilla
1-1/2 cups milk
2 cups all-purpose flour

2 cups of sugar
1/2 cup of unsweetened cocoa
   powder
2 teaspoons baking powder
2 teaspoons baking soda
1/2 teaspoon of salt
1 box of red hot candies

Sift together dry ingredients. Add wet ingredients beating in eggs last. Mix thoroughly with a hand mixer on low speed. Bake in two round cake pans at 350 degrees for 25–30 minutes or until a broom straw stuck in the middle of the cake comes out clean. Cool. Frost with white butter frosting. Decorate with red hot candies.

## White Butter Frosting

3 cups confectioners' sugar sifted twice
2 tablespoons of milk
1/3 cup unsalted butter, at room temp
1 teaspoon of vanilla extract

Mix together sugar and butter till crumbly. Add milk and vanilla, mixing with a hand-held mixer on low speed.

"Your mama had a pretty reading voice. While the cake was baking she used to read to me from one of her dream books."

"What dream books?" My ears are suddenly alert.

"She used to make up the prettiest stories. All kinds of fairy tales and dreams. She used to make up dreams and write them down in a little blue notebook that fit in the pocket of her dress. That child had the most vivid imagination. She said big words use to chase her in her dreams and when she stabbed them they wouldn't bleed. Imagine that," Aunt Faith says and starts rocking, holding on to her stomach as if it is a baby in her arms. She is quiet for a while, remembering. Her stomach growls, breaking the silence.

"You could use Sweet'n Low instead of sugar in the cake. You probably couldn't tell the difference," she says. She licks her lips as if she can taste the sting of the red hot candies on her tongue, feel the buttery frosting slick on her lips.

She sounds like a little girl. I can't resist. I decide right then that soon, I will bake her a red velvet cake and decorate the top with little red hot candies in the shape of a heart because it means I love you and I do love her.

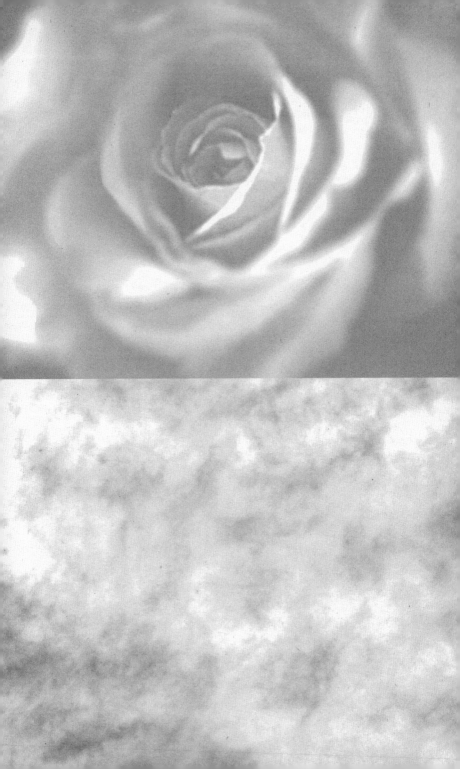

FOURTEEN

*M*atisse calls a few times after I'm back in Georgia, but the sound of his suffering is bad weather to my ears. I am afraid to talk to him, because I don't yet know how to answer when he asks me to come back. I rub the homemade tattoo on my thigh so that it will bring tears to my eyes. I think I'm supposed to be sad but I'm not.

I see the ivory envelope, long and wide, lying on the dining-room table. His wild script turns my name into abstract initials. He never writes letters, he says they will betray him. The paintings he sends me tell the story. His feelings for me are transparent. His love is like an open wound. I open the envelope and pull out the picture sandwiched between two heavy pieces of cardboard. I stack it with the others in a shoebox I keep under my bed. I try to forget, but I can't. I feel the sweep of his eyes and his silent caresses and the memory of them makes me itch in the lap of my satin slip.

*T*he door to the big white house is open, the hallway empty, but heavy with the scent of lilacs. I step from the warmth of the strong summer sunlight into the parlor and am swallowed by deep, rich, thick shades of burgundy and wine.

"Who's there?" Aunt Faith stands like a tree in the doorway behind me.

"Mariah."

She walks over to me leaning on her cane. When she is so close I can smell the peppermint on her breath, her hands fly to my face, her cloudy sightless eyes look into my startled ones. I touch her hand and she steps closer. We are belly to belly. She cups my face in her large, smooth hands and slowly travels every road on my face and figure.

"You're healthy. Soft skin. Strong arms. Wide hips." She slaps me playfully on my ass. She is acting like my mama. I want to be more like a daughter. I wrap my arms around her wide middle and sink into the welcome of her body.

"You'll make some man happy on your wedding night." She laughs. So do I, knowing like her I'll never marry.

Late that night I hear music and the sound of finger popping. I tiptoe down the stairs and sit on the bottom landing. Aunt Faith is in the parlor singing along and finger popping to Pinetop Perkins.

"Come on in, we having a party," she says, sitting in the big red rocking chair snapping her fingers and tapping her feet.

Just me and Aunt Faith. I pull her to her feet and we dance the hootchie-cootchie, twist and shout, bump, and cakewalk until sweat stings our eyes. She is a slim young woman in a yellow party dress and I am her dapper escort, aroused in the presence of a pretty girl dipping her narrow hips so low to the floor.

*Down to the river/Down to the river I'm bound/My girl need a man to go down/Down to the river for a drink of honey wine.*

We sing along with the lyrics and let our bodies keep time.

Aunt Faith reminds me to to wear a hat when it's cold out, to take an umbrella when her knees tell her it's going to rain. She says prayers for me, plays records for me when I am sad. She takes care of me, treats me like her own, and I like it, grow used to her love. I read aloud to her from books by the black writers—Ann Petry, Alice Walker, Toni Morrison, James Baldwin, and Toni Cade Bambara—I have newly discovered in the school library. She doesn't always like what I read to her, but she is always appreciative. She waits patiently for me to finish reading what I have chosen before asking me to end the evening with a reading from a book of bible stories her mother read to her when she was a child.

Aunt Faith asks me about the letters I get every week from my father. Sometimes I wonder if my life with Matisse ever existed. I avoid her questions and reveal as little as possible.

One day Matisse calls me to say that he has sold two paintings.

"I'll be in a group show next month," he says, trying to sound happy.

"That's good." I don't know what else to say. There is silence for a while. I think of asking him about the weather in Los Angeles, but I know it's always the same.

"Have you seen Mrs. Oyama?"

"No. Not anymore." He pauses. "When are you coming back?" he asks, catching me off guard.

"Aunt Faith is sick."

"We could be a family." He sounds as if he has forgotten how miserably we failed.

"Which paintings did you sell?" I ask, picking at a pimple on my arm, trying to make it bleed. He says nothing for a while. I can hear his ragged breathing. I can't bear to tell him, but I know I will never go back. It is too dangerous for us to travel that road again.

"I love you," he says. Then he hangs up the phone.

Time passes slowly. Weeks into months of sleeping and drinking grief with a short-handled spoon. One day I find a dusty bottle of whiskey in a corner of the kitchen cupboard and I discover a new recipe for erasing memory.

*There is an October window in the room. An old tea-stained lace curtain filters the effort of the sunlight. Through the dirty yellow panes, I see the true blue of the sky, filled with clouds and the tips of trees in flames. Autumn leaves dance in the air like wishes. Matisse is painting my thighs with his tongue and I am coming in my dreams.*

I pack up the box of paintings, pictures, and obsessive expressions of love my father has sent me over the weeks we have been apart and mail it all back to him with a note. *Daddy, You love me too much. Mariah.*

Each picture is a pain in my heart, each cryptic poem reveals his devotion to my missing mother, and the crack in my broken heart deepens each time the mail carrier arrives with a tear-stained package. When I look at the photograph of Matisse standing shirtless in front of the ocean I see my father, but when I remember him late at night

I see a man whose needs are too great. I am aware of my body and in the dark I am ashamed of my thoughts. *My dreams do not lie.*

When Matisse calls me a week later his desperation is static on the line. Aunt Faith is taking a nap and I am standing in front of the refrigerator wondering what I will cook for supper. The phone rings three times before I pick it up.

"Hello," I say. There is silence. "Is anyone there?" A heavy sigh blows like a foreign wind in my ear.

"I want to be a good father to you," he says firmly.

In the silence I draw circles with my finger on the wall.

"You're right. It's too much. I'm sorry . . ." He waits for me but I don't help. "What do you want most? If you could have anything?" he asks.

I breathe into the phone, but I cannot speak.

"I want to make you happy. I'll do anything to make you happy," he says, choking on the words. It hurts me to hear him cry.

"Call me if you need anything. I'll always be here for you." He pauses and says, "I love you." We both hang up at the same time.

Maybe when we're strangers again we'll understand better how to be who we are.

That night I dream about my mother.

*I lift the curtains from the window to see her staring at me. Her closely cropped blonde afro, her almond eyes lined in silver. She has grown plump, more frail than I remember. She is wearing a strapless satin sea-blue dress that looks like it was sewn onto her body. She stands on the porch in her bare feet, her dusty shoes dangling from her left hand. A small black suitcase sits behind her on the porch. I open the door and stand across the threshold from her, wondering if I should let her in. I close my eyes to hold back my tears and press my hand to my mouth to keep from screaming.*

*"There you are," she says.*

*Her voice is soft, sad, and sweet like each one of my memories. The sound of my mother's voice is like honey to my ears. My hungry eyes drink her up, swell and rain. She takes a step foward and offers me a word. I hesitate, but the gravity of my longing makes me fall into her arms. She is warm and smells like the inside of a flower. In her arms I grow sleepy. My arms are tired, but I am afraid to let her go; when I do, I am surprised that I do not fall.*

*Solo sueños.* I am only dreaming.
*Solo sueños.*

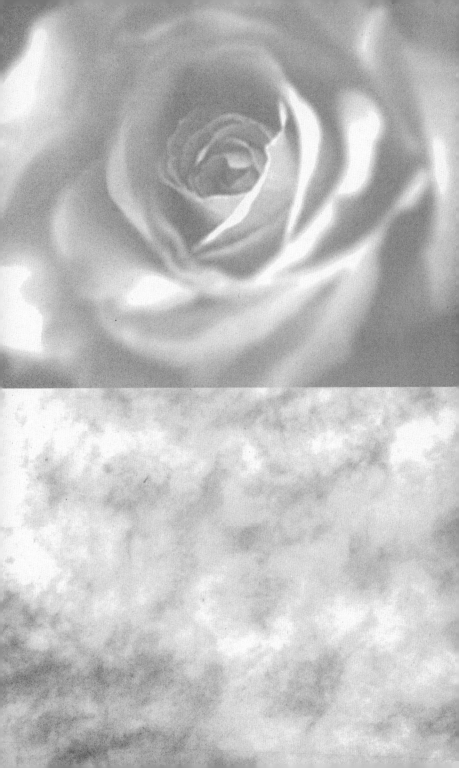

FIFTEEN

The ugly white modern buildings of the college are clustered together on several acres of green hilly land like discarded building blocks, but the library is a two-story sturdy red brick structure that looks like someone's home. It sits like a proud island in the center of the campus, dressed defiantly in a thick drape of dark green ivy, white shutters, and a gray slate roof. In my first year at the college seven miles from the big white house, I get the perfect job of shelving books. The librarian is a kind, older woman in her sixties, Mrs. Walters, who wears a black linty headband around her short blond hair and dresses in very unlibrarianlike bright colors and low-heeled white patent-leather pumps every day. She walks on her toes so as not to make noise when she walks across the room.

"I remember when blacks were not allowed to take classes in English and engineering. Oh, it was not said aloud, but it was discouraged as impractical. I hope that you will take classes in all the things that interest you, my dear. I'm glad to have been able to see so many changes in my lifetime." She speaks at me as if she doesn't expect an answer so I keep shelving books. Mostly she leaves me to my secret pleasures.

Working in the school library, I slip between the pages of books as if I am naked and they ease my flesh. I collect words each day from books so new I crack their spines and volumes so old the delicate paper holds on to my fingerprints. I write new words on the walls of my bedroom at night, stringing them together into pyramids, trees, and tribes, inventing a new way to manage language and a new life inside the poetry of rhythm and rhyme, straight lines and lines that curl into expressions beneath the palms of my hand. Soon the words begin to escape from the walls, becoming bigger and bolder and stretching toward the ceiling. I begin to write poetry in a blue notebook that fits in my pocket.

I take classes in French. *Mon père est un homme triste.* My father is a sad man. I miss him. Music Appreciation. Brahms is a lullaby that hushes my cries before I sleep. My dreams disturb me. History. Every day I sit next to white girls who ask to see my notes and white boys who ask me for my phone number. Black girls are suspicious of my proper ways and attitude. Black boys call me sister and ask me to come with them to political meetings. I ignore them all, knowing that sooner or later they'll ask me questions I don't want to entertain. I amuse myself. I twist long difficult words into glossy silk ropes that I wear around my waist at night.

I study these new subjects by the light of one of Aunt Merleen's handcarved lamps, from time to time sipping from teacups full of bourbon and honey. Alone in my bed at night, I introduce my hands to my body. In the dark, when I no longer hear the finger popping, I unbutton my nightshirt and open my thighs against the cool dark wood. Rosemary smoothes the ragged edges of the whiskey. We play our silent melodies until I fall asleep in her embrace. My dreams are coded, I only remember the feelings, not the images. Mostly I wake up feeling as if I have been drained, then tossed away, like an empty drinking glass.

And then one day after I have already taken a bend in the road Aunt Faith delivers to me a fresh reminder that death is nearby always.

"Your grandmother Gert died this morning," she says across the kitchen table decorated with measuring cups and spoons, flour, eggs, sugar, blue ceramic mixing bowls, and a bottle of red dye.

My first thought is that I am relieved that I no longer have to go to the nursing home after church on Sundays. My next thought is what makes me forget the three new words I have to write on my walls; it is the possibility of my mother coming home for the funeral.

"How will Mama know? Do you think she'll come home?"

"I called somebody who knows where to reach her. They said she'll come for the funeral," Aunt Faith says, as if breaking worse news after bad. "In a day or two."

I don't want to believe her. I wish I did not want this so much. I untie the apron at my waist and turn off the oven. Aunt Faith's red velvet cake will have to wait. I walk down the hallway as I have done each time she has sent word over the years. I sit and stare at the light filtering through the thin curtains at the window by the door and I try to fast-forward to the part where she is holding me close, kissing me for the hundredth time. Although I am past the age of reason and know that she was wrong to leave me, I can't seem to move from the spot at the bottom of the stairs where I've waited for her all these years.

I drive Aunt Faith to the nursing home to claim Grandmother Gert's belongings. For the first time since I've come back I go inside with her leaning on me, letting me guide her through the heavy glass doors, down the long white hallway to the room where Gert no doubt used her last breath to curse somebody out. All of her things fit into a large green plastic bag. A brand-new purple silk dressing gown, five flowered house dresses with *Gertrude Rains* written in the collar in black Magic Marker, a small stack of underwear, a small box of costume jewelry, and a couple of lap robes. Just as I am about to close the drawer in the table next to her bed I see a photograph stuck in the back corner. It is of my mother as a small girl sitting on my grandmother's lap. In the photograph they are both smiling. I slip the photograph into my pocket and guide Faith back to the car.

I drive Aunt Faith to the funeral home where I mechanically make the arrangements for the funeral. The funeral director is a slight, well-dressed older woman in a dark gray suit, who fingers the small gold hoop earring in her right ear and carries a miniature white Bible in her left hand. She presses her hand to the small of my back and tries to comfort me.

"Your aunt is lucky to have such a devoted niece. This must be terribly difficult for you," she says.

Aunt Faith sits in the corner and cries. I try to focus on the insurance papers and casket types and flower arrangements, although I don't care about such things. This nice lady can put her in a cardboard box, barbecue her, and set off fireworks for all I care. Mama is heavy on my mind.

Later that evening to keep myself occupied, to ease Aunt Faith's pain, and to welcome my mother home, I begin again to bake the red velvet cake. I light the oven. Aunt Faith is second cook, giving me verbal instructions on mixing and beating and baking, and when the three rounds are done we let them cool on wire racks near the window. I frost the two-layer cake while Aunt Faith runs her plump fingers around the edges of the batter bowl. I lather icing on the third smaller round of cake so that we can perform a taste test. Aunt Faith eats pieces of the red velvet cake delicately with both hands reaching for her mouth. She hums in approval and licks the frosting from her fingers.

I almost drop the cake when the phone rings. I rush to pick it up in the hallway hoping I will recognize the voice and I do, it is Tree. I can hear Joy's children crying in the background.

"I'm sorry about your grandmother," Tree says loudly over the noise.

"Thank you for calling," I say automatically. I don't want to talk to her or to anyone just now and hurry off the phone.

*M*y mother does not come for the funeral. I am thirsty for a sip of something that will burn my throat down to my belly.

Only one nurse from the nursing home, a new one, comes to the chapel. We follow the hearse to the cemetery. Aunt Faith is crying and moaning as if her sister Gertrude Rains were not the most spiteful, mean, and nasty person when she was alive. I don't understand her sorrow until I remember that it wasn't so long ago that she'd had to do this all by herself for Merleen. I cried for them then, but this fresh grief is for my mother. Tears begin to flow from my eyes like small pieces of broken glass as I guide Aunt Faith off the path. We walk past Grandma Gert's prepared grave, passing headstones overrun with weeds or decorated with plastic flowers and flowery quotes. *Our dear father. Sister and friend. Loving mother* is written in large beautiful script on a pink marble headstone near the big black gate surrounding the cemetery. Suddenly I am pulling out my hair and the nurse has to hold my hands away from the destruction.

My mother may as well be dead. Her eyes and organs gone to dust. I don't know whether to run or hide, I am paralyzed. I am irritable, don't go to class or to my job at the library and I stop combing my hair.

I say mean things to Aunt Faith but most of the time I ignore her.

"You're so quiet, what's wrong, Mariah?"

"Does something have to be wrong? I just don't feel like talking about insignificant things." I know I've hurt her feelings but I don't care. Her voice reminds me that I'm alive. Words begin to drip from the ceiling onto my head. Big words, heavy sentences, and pages from old newspapers fall on my face and melt like rain. I become afraid to leave the house. I am afraid if I go out into the light, I could lose my life, afraid my voice will disappear into the trees, my eyes will be eaten by tiny insects in the air, my mouth torn loose by fingers reaching from passing cars. I am afraid that if I go outside, screams will fly from my throat and fall like hollow trees in a valley of echoes. I am afraid of everything. Nothing is real. Nothing is as it seems. I refuse to leave my room. When the honey that sweetens the liquor is gone, I drink what is left of the bourbon straight from the bottle until it is empty.

Through the pillows of thick gray fog, I hear a faint knocking at my door. It is irritating. I want to sleep forever.

"Mariah?" Aunt Faith asks. I don't answer, but she keeps knocking.

"Mariah? Child, open the door." Her voice is grating, pushing through the dense layers of clouds.

I pull the covers over my head and turn over in the tangle of sheets. I put my hands over my ears. The door opens, then the curtains, the windows open wide. The sunlight doesn't melt my skin, the fresh air doesn't burn. Aunt Faith makes her way to the bed and lets her enormous weight crush the mattress with a sigh.

"Talk to your Aunt Faith. Talk to me, baby."

I want to answer her, but I can't find my tongue, it seems lost in my mouth. I feel Aunt Faith's hands on my back. Her fingers crawl up my arm to my face. She pulls my body towards her until my face is leaned against her heavy, peppermint-scented chest.

*There is peace in the valley . . .* She is singing hymns softly into my ear.

*Once upon a time, a long time ago, when I was a railman's daughter . . .* She is breathing the words of a story into my chest.

*Got my mojo working . . .* She is finger popping to Muddy Waters.

"Water," I whisper. "Water."

Aunt Faith pushes off the bed, bringing me with her. With her cane in one hand and me in the other she guides us down the hall and into the bathroom. She half drags me to the sink in the corner of the room. She turns on the faucet. It sounds like a river. I cup my hands under the stream of cool water and I drink an ocean. The sweet taste of water kills my thirst. Tears spring from my fingertips, my hair, the crease in my elbow, from my knees and from between my toes. Aunt Faith holds me.

She walks me to her room and sits me on her bed. Cool, smooth cotton. I hear a river. Her hands undress me. When I am naked, she leads me to the bath. The water is hot. My skin tingles as my body is swallowed by the long, deep tub. Aunt Faith sprinkles a handful of herbs into the water, rose petals, and a tablespoon full of honey. It smells delicious. She hums an old blues tune as she rubs rough sea salt into my back and shoulders. I am swimming in a savory soup.

She lights a white candle and we wait. She sits down wearily in a chair facing me. She rests her hands on her big belly and watches me with her cloudy eyes. She is listening to me.

Before I know what is happening, words begin to spill out of my mouth like snakes. Words fly from my throat like birds. I spit out every detail like poison. I leave out nothing.

*The things I miss*

My mother's breasts . . . the weight of Aunt Merleen's hand in mine . . .

*The things I lost*

My innocence . . .

*The things I want . . .*

Love . . . Arms I can trust to hold me . . .

Alone in my room that night, I write down the last word my mother gave me. *Water.* I lift the edge of the paper to my lips and I drink it off the page, swallow it in two long syllables until it meets the place that is burning as brightly as day. It is as if the weight of a thousand stones has been lifted from my chest. I am light as a page in a blank book. I feel empty, but somehow whole. My mouth opens and I speak to people who remember me and greet strangers with a smile. The sun comes out and the grass is green again and the taste of water is sweet. I write poems and draw maps of language.

Mama still calls from time to time and speaks to Aunt Faith, but I no longer stop stirring pots, folding sheets, or writing poems to sit by the door waiting for the sound of her coming. I've decided to keep moving.

When she comes through the door I will drink her up in long greedy swallows. I remember each word my mother gave me and I savor the taste of her soul kisses.

*Sweet Blue Music*
*Whispers*
*Dream Water*
*Rain Rusty Tears*

My thirst is endless, the well has no bottom, but there is love around me, I'm sure of it now.

## *Acknowledgments*

Gratitude and thanks:

To the Yaddo family for a place at the table and a room of my own; Charis Books & More in Atlanta for encouraging me to come out as a writer and supporting my efforts always; the City of Atlanta Bureau of Cultural Affairs for a Mayor's Award in Literature; the Georgia Council on the Arts and the Astraea Foundation for generous grants that gave me the treasured gift of time.

To my agent Sandy Dijkstra and the extraordinary staff at the Dijkstra Literary Agency, especially Debra Ginsberg, for believing in the promise of a few seeds; my editor Julie Grau, whose confidence and editorial talents were invaluable; and Nicole Wan, her compassionate assistant.

To Ann Khaddar and Eric Broudy for allowing poetry in the workplace; Brown University Food Services for feeding my body and soul with small and large acts of kindness; Irene Zahava for generously editing an early version of the manuscript with care; Daniel Alexander Jones for luminescent soul kisses; Marj Salvodon for regular, edifying e-mail; my assistant Nina Shope for great timing; and the Soul Sister's Salon Divas, Kate Rushin, Carleasa Coates, Rebecca Johnson, Patricia Powell, and Meredith Woods for the power of their words.

This work would not have been possible without the loving support of numerous friends and family in Atlanta, Boston, Hawaii, London, Los Angeles, Minneapolis/St. Paul, New York, Paris, Providence, San Francisco, Brown University, and Wheaton College.

Grace and thanks to all of you, for everything.

## About the Author

Shay Youngblood was born in Columbus, Georgia, and received her B.A. from Clark Atlanta University and an M.F.A. from Brown University. She is a playwright (*Shakin' the Mess Outta Misery* and *Talking Bones*) and the author of a story collection, *The Big Mama Stories,* one of which was awarded a Pushcart Prize.